BRIDGE OVER TIME

Book Cover by:
SelfPubBookcovers.com/sarabooks

A NOVEL BY: LINDA MAYO

COPYWRITE : 07/04/2017

BRIDGE OVER TIME

By Linda Mayo
Copyright 2017 by Linda Mayo
All Rights Reserved

Published by Linda Mayo
Printed in the United States Of America
Copyright @2017 Linda Mayo
ISBN: 978-0-692-95878-0
Cover design by: www.SelfPubbookcovers.com

BRIDGE OVER TIME
WRITTEN BY: LINDA MAYO
TABLE OF CONTENTS

CHAPTER 1	THE MANOR	PG 4
CHAPTER 2	THE 100TH ANNIVERSARY	PG 12
CHAPTER 3	THE CONTACT	PG 17
CHAPTER 4	THE HISTORY	PG 24
CHAPTER 5	COMPARING CONTACTS	PG 27
CHAPTER 6	CELESTE'S REVEAL	PG 32
CHAPTER 7	THE DECISION	PG 38
CHAPTER 8	THE WEDDING	PG43
CHAPTER 9	RETURN WITH NO PARENTS	PG 50
CHAPTER 10	SETTLING IN	PG 55
CHAPTER 11	THE REUNION	PG 60
CHAPTER 12	RETURN TO LOVE	PG 72
CHAPTER 13	A TINY GIFT	PG 77
CHAPTER 14	BABY MAKES THREE	PG 81
CHAPTER 15	TIL DEATH DO US PART	PG 88
CHAPTER 16	LIFE WITHOUT EDWARD	PG 98
CHAPTER 17	RETURN TO REALITY	PG 108
CHAPTER 18	CONFUSED LOVE	PG 118
CHAPTER 19	FACING HER FEARS	PG 133
CHAPTER 20	WHAT IS THE NEW NORMAL?	PG 141
CHAPTER 21	ALL IN A DAYS WORK	PG 150
CHAPTER 22	BREATHTAKING	PG 156
CHAPTER 23	THEN COMES MARRIAGE	PG 160
CHAPTER 24	WEDDING SURPRISE	PG 167
CHAPTER 25	BRIDGING TIME	PG 173

CHAPTER 1

THE MANOR

As Bridgette pulls into the long driveway, she is struck by the beauty of the majestic marble mansion. The Italian historic manor with its tall pillars and columns is breath-taking. She feels an attraction to the structure since reading so many stories about its history. Stories told of a husband who built it for his beautiful wife in the early 1900's, a love story remembered through the ages, a concept she finds romantic and endearing. The current owner of the manor is holding an open-house today in celebration of its 100th year. During this event, he hopes to attract a buyer. He has aged and plans to rid himself of his assets. With no heirs, he intends to leave everything to his business partner, a close friend for many years.

Bridgette's reason for coming to see the manor is the history behind it, and her knowledge of the owners that originally built the structure. Her great, great grandmother was once the owner of this magnificent place. Her fascination with the manor is relentless. She notices as she drives up the long driveway leading to the front of the massive structure that she is the only one in the driveway. She double-checks the appointment confirmation for date and time. Finding the date and time correct, she thinks it strange there are no other vehicles for the tour. She especially thinks it's odd that her appointment is made for this time of day, since today is the celebration of the manor. She assumed that an appointment was needed to attend the celebration for headcount. With no one in sight, she gets out of her car and approaches the entrance.

The towering mahogany doors appear gigantic before her as she approaches. Touching the large handle, she presses the lever down to open. Pushing hard on the door, she feels its heaviness and the bulk of its size. She walks into a spacious area where a large grand stairway looms directly in front of her. The steps are wide, reaching straight up to a beautiful stained-glass window centered at the top of the landing. New steps begin on each side of the landing to continue up to the next level. As she gazes at the stained-glass window, she catches the shadow of a woman leaving the main stairs to continue up the right side of the stairway.

"Hello," Bridgette speaks loud enough for the woman to hear.

At the same moment, a gentleman approaches her from an entryway on her right.

"Hello," she speaks again, but in a lower voice. "I apologize for yelling. I saw someone on the landing just entering the second set of stairs."

The gentleman pauses, then looks up to the empty landing at the top of the wide stairs. He says, "I only have one reservation for this morning, I didn't hear anyone come in."

"I thought I saw a woman walking up the stairs," Bridgette tells him quickly brushing it aside.

"No," he states slowly, examining her now with a more direct gaze, as if pondering. There is something about her face that is familiar. Dismissing that thought, he continues, "I'm the only person here. I've been waiting in the room next door. No one has entered but you, at least not that I have seen."

"I thought today was the celebration of over 100 years of Celestial Manor? This place should be swamped with people," she says with curiosity.

"The celebration begins later today. No appointment needed for that," he asserts now recognizing her confusion. "I apologize if you were misled with the time details."

"No that's okay, it was most likely my mistake. I requested the appointment, not realizing the celebration was later in the day and that an appointment wasn't needed."

He ask, "Do you still wish to have the personal tour? Of course there will be no charge since you were confused with the details."

Bridgette nods yes.

He says smiling, "Let's begin your tour then." As he motions for her to step this way, he begins the prepared dialogue for the tour.

She watches him and decides he is probably as old as the house. His demeanor is stately, a formality she decides is indicative of the time period of his assumed age. His tall thin statured frame reminds her of a soldier at attention. His stiffness seems to soften as he shows genuine sincerity when he speaks of the mansion.

His smile continues as, he announces with a formal tone, "My name is Victor. I am the guide for Celestial Manor, and I have been a guide here for many years. The manor was built in the early 1900's by Edward Harrington, a successful businessman from New York. He relocated to Virginia at the urging of his lovely wife, Celeste, for whom he named the manor. Her father's career brought him to Virginia regularly. He fell in love with the area, making the decision to move the family south when he retired. Being of prominent stature, Celeste's father could afford the luxuries of the day so he purchased an estate in Afton. When Edward brought Celeste to visit her family, she fell in love with the beauty of the countryside. Wishing to be near her family, her husband considered properties close by. Celeste's father, who wanted his daughter close, showed this parcel of land to Edward, cultivating the idea of a summer home. The view is panoramic in every direction atop a beautiful mountain. It was easy for Edward to say yes for Celeste. It took two years to build the mansion structure due to the marble hauled in from distant locations. Each detail of the property was carefully designed solely by Edward."

Victor speaks of each room and its contents as they walk the lower floor. The main living area is decorated with thick velvet burgundy drapes, modern in the early 1900s. The furniture is made of dark mahogany wood, decorated with embroidered burgundy and gold material. It goes well with the matching mantle and the wood trim of the room, both elegant and regal.

They walk the dining area with its long wooden table and matching cushioned seats. The curtains, unlike the main area are gold in this room. In the center of each end of the table are two short gold candelabras with six small white candles placed strategically for lighting. She doesn't see the kitchen, but Victor shows Bridgette a butler's door where the food was placed to be brought up by a dumbwaiter from the kitchen on the floor below. The meals were topped with dome covers and transported to this floor by the pulley shaft. The china cabinet still holds the lovely original dinnerware. In the corner of the room, an easel stands with an enlarged picture of the table setting for an evening. Bridgette stares at it. She has the distinct eerie feeling she has been seated at this table before.

Next, they enter what Victor refers to as the Gentleman's Room. The men would retire to this room after dinner to smoke a pipe and enjoy conversations of their independent businesses. Victor explains that many a deal could have happened in this room. It has small single tier tables beside each leathered chair, where ashes were emptied into hand-crafted trays. On the corner of the ash trays are several dented sections, the size of a pipe's bowl, where a pipe is placed once it has been smoked. The décor is masculine with four large leather chairs facing a fireplace on the center of one wall. Overhead hangs a metal wrought iron sculpted design with curves in all directions posing as a chandelier. Victor explains that it was handmade by a blacksmith. The room has a lavatory adjacent.

Making their way to the large staircase, Bridgette looks up at the striking stained-glass window. Approaching the window at the top of the stairs, Victor informs Bridgette that Edward designed this window. "The woman in the glass is in his wife's image."

Standing in front of the stained glass, Bridgette can see the woman's face matches her own. No matter where Bridgette stands, the penetrating eyes are looking back at her. They seem to follow her as she moves. Bridgette, totally captivated says, "It's beautiful!" Her brown hair with auburn highlights brings out the piercing gray blue eyes that are mesmerizing. Taking in the image, it shows Celeste's hair cascading down her back and over her right shoulder. As Bridgette stares at the image, Victor tells her that when you are outside, it appears as if she is looking at the luscious landscape surrounding the mansion. She is captured from a side view, looking out the window, yet when you are inside, it appears as if her eyes meet yours. The glass has a riveting design and uniqueness. There is something about the portrait that makes Bridgette linger immersed in its details. On each side of the window are etched glass doors. Victor pushes on one. To Bridgette's surprise, the doors lead to a large open balcony that overlooks ponds and garden statues. Sculpted stone planters are placed all around the edges of the balcony filled with delicate flowers of the season. He points to the glass window. Celeste is watching her again.

They return to the stairwell landing inside. The tour continues to the next set of steps around a corner post, the same stairway she had witnessed the woman climb earlier. The handrails are mahogany with sculpted black wrought-iron design that meets the mahogany bottom rail. The mere look of it suggests great wealth. The steps go directly up to a long hallway where other giant doors give way to large quarters with stylishly decorated eighteenth-century furnishings. Every room has its own suite complete with fireplace and lavatory. It's surprising, she thinks, that it has electricity. At that moment, Victor explains that this was the first place in the area that had electricity. "Edward spared no expense by putting a power house right on the property to provide for the enormous demand." He says these words with great admiration. He takes her from room to room giving details behind every selection of décor. Each room has its own design with coordinating features. Some are regal, others masculine, and others are specifically designed for femininity and delicate trinkets. The posh settings are lavish with expensive; and extravagant details.

Victor and Bridgette enter what he refers to as the master suite. "Celeste and Edward had been to Italy. They stayed in a charming villa where Celeste fell in love with the décor. She designed this room closely resembling the one they had stayed in on their honeymoon. The large bed with its four tall posts, have intricate designs carved into the wood. The armoire was made of the same wood as the posts, with matching carved designs. Mr. and Mrs. Harrington had exquisite tastes as shown by the lavish furnishings here. This room is neither feminine nor masculine." He ends this portion of the tour by saying, "Celeste died in this room in 1923."

That information jolts her! Bridgette turns her head quickly as she sees a shadow pass by the doorway in the hall. "There she is, the woman I saw on the steps just passed the doorway."

Victor excuses himself and walks out into the hallway. "Hello, the tour is in here," he exclaims yelling down the hall. He continues his search looking in each room as he scans the hallways.

While he is out of the room, Bridgette moves around inspecting the items on display, touching things gently. In the distance, she hears a low soft woman's voice say, "I'm so glad you are finally here." Bridgette turns swiftly, but sees no one. She's startled, and when Victor returns, she frantically asks, "Did you hear that?"

Victor replies quizzically, "Hear what? I found no one in the hall."

"It was a woman's voice speaking very low. She said she was glad I was finally here!" Bridgette repeats what she heard feeling anxious.

Victor sees her discomfort and responds to her, "No, I'm sorry I didn't hear it. Are you sure that's what you heard? These old walls creak and make a lot of noise."

"Yes, I know that's what I heard."

Calmly, he takes her by the arm and they walk out into the hallway. He tries to reassure her by making light of it. He says, "It must be a ghost," immediately scolding himself internally for saying such a stupid thing.

She quickly looks up at him searching for sincerity of that statement.

He smiles at her and gives a chuckle trying to lighten the moment. "Let's go outside to see the gardens and waterfalls." Taking her by the elbow, he leads her to a staircase that leads back toward the stained-glass window.

As she passes, she watches the woman's face in the glass looking back at her. Their eyes meet, and she finds it difficult to move past it. She stops and envelopes the gaze between them.

Victor continues walking down the large center staircase that leads back down to the foyer, but stops when he notices she's not behind him. He glances up the staircase to see an image of Celeste standing behind Bridgette looking in his direction. He panics when he sees the unnerving image! He sees that Celeste and Bridgette are exact images of each other. Why hadn't he seen it before? He screams in utter hysteria. "My God, I knew you were in this house. I knew it!"

Startled by the comment, Bridgette looks down at Victor with questionable concern. "What?"

The image becomes transparent as Victor rushes up the steps to Bridgette. As the figure fades, he takes Bridgette's arm and hurries her down the steps. "Let's continue the tour of the grounds," he says trying to pretend the sighting and his words never happened. He rushes her outside.

Once outside, she takes a deep breath inhaling the fresh air. She admits to a moment of panic upstairs, and to be honest felt quite vulnerable. Something made her feel tense and uneasy in that house, yet simultaneously drawn to its mystery. She asks Victor, "What did you see?"

The reputation of the manor needs above all to be protected. Any announcement of ghosts could alter any prospect of a sale so he decides to down-play his observation. "The image of you beside Celeste was captivating, as if she was still alive. Your reflection mingled with hers on the glass, as if you were the same person," he tells her covering his emotions storming inside.

She accepts this explanation and tries to brush it aside.

The tour continues with no other unexplainable events. The grounds are just as scenic and beautiful as the internal features of the home. The statued fountains are of Greek design, breaking away from the Italian splendor. Covered walkways lead to more glorious views of the valley. Turning to gaze at the house, she has a moment of Deja vu. Everything seems so familiar.

Wrapping up the tour by entering the main lobby again, Victor provides her with a brochure detailing other tour dates and the history of the manor. He thanks her for coming and escorts her through the large mahogany doors. They part ways with a handshake indicating the tour has come to its conclusion. She walks down the steps toward her parked car in the drive, and turns taking one more look at the large massive home. She again sees the woman standing in front of a window on the second floor. I knew I had seen her, she thinks as she opens her car door to get in. Why is she being so evasive? She starts her car and drives down the lengthy driveway to leave the manor that drew her in from the moment she had arrived. What she had not told Victor was that her great, great grandmother was Celeste, who had died long before she was born.

CHAPTER 2

THE 100th CELEBRATION

The big celebration event is in full swing by one o'clock in the afternoon. People are in line waiting to enter the manor house. Victor isn't used to seeing so many people roaming through the house, it's usually filled with silence. The manor is open for anyone to walk freely from room to room today. There are tour guides in every room to deliver a prepared speech, answer questions and to protect the estate's valuables. As Victor walks through the main quarters, he finds no alarming events to concern him. The earlier vision of Celeste has left him a bit unnerved. He is mulling over in his head whether to tell the owner about Celeste's appearance. The two had discussed the possibility of it being haunted before, but neither had seen what Victor had seen today. He wonders to himself if today's activities have something to do with it. Was the date significant? Was the date awakening a long sleeping ghost, or did it have something to do with Bridgette, the nine o'clock appointment? He thought to himself the words Bridgette had said, "I am glad you are finally here." He wishes now he had questioned her about her family history. Maybe there is a long-lost connection in her heritage that Celeste knows. Without more information, he could only speculate. He has her contact information so he decides to contact her another day to probe more about her family. The thing that strikes him is the resemblance she holds to Celeste. The two standing side-by-side, show strong similarities.

Guests are coming and going all day. The owner, Mr. Barkley, is busy with various investors trying to interest them in the purchase of the property. Unfortunately for him, no one seems to be interested enough to take on such a large investment. Most hadn't a clue what they would do with this enormous manor. The upkeep costs alone would be astronomical, not to mention there are some needed repairs, things that would be costly.

Toward the end of the day, a prospective gentleman walks in leaving Victor with last minute hopes of a purchaser. The visitor walks through the halls with purpose, as if he knows each room. Victor approaches introducing himself, and probes with questions trying to gauge his interest.

Entering the master suite, Victor asserts, "Gorgeous, don't you agree? Hello, my name is Victor," he holds out his hand to shake the visitor's hand.

"Yes," he replies with a side-glance toward Victor while roaming the room. "Oh sorry, my name is Jason." He turns back to shake Victor's hand. "This place is enormous."

"Yes," Victor replies. "It has twenty rooms that encompass an astounding 23,000 square feet."

"Wow! That's big! No one lives here?" Jason asks.

"No sir. Not at this time."

"It's a shame, it feels like home," Jason shares while still perusing the area.

When Jason had barely made the statement of home, Victor hears simultaneously, "Edward." He turns to see Celeste staring at Jason.

"My Edward," she repeats again staring at Jason lovingly.

Victor searches for Jason's reaction but sees none. Victor turns and excuses himself promptly beginning to feel the rush of panic pouring over him. She has appeared for the second time today! He needs to speak to the owner, so he rushes down the steps to find him. We have a problem that will cause this house not to sell, not to mention he's afraid to be in this house anymore.

He makes it back to the main level where he sees Mr. Barkley speaking with guests. He walks up, excuses himself to the members, and asks for a minute of Mr. Barkley's time.

"What is it Victor? You look upset," Mr. Barkley suggests after they walk away from the guests.

"Mr. Barkley, we have a ghost in this house."

"I know, Victor. We have discussed this before."

"No. I mean she is here right now! I just saw her in the master suite. She is calling a visitor, 'Edward'."

Mr. Barkley asks with incredulous disbelief, "What?"

"I'm not kidding. I have seen her twice today. Earlier this morning I gave a tour for a young woman, and Celeste appeared right before my eyes. The visitor was standing in front of the window at the top of the stairs. I continued down the steps, and when I turned back, Celeste was standing behind the young woman. I swear to you, they could have been twins. They looked so much alike! Then, just now, a guest was walking through the master suite and Celeste appeared staring at the guest calling him Edward."

Victor is visibly shaken and unnerved.

"Okay, Okay, let's go. I want to see her for myself," Mr. Barkley says, thinking all the while this is unbelievable. All the way up to the room he's talking to Victor. "Why would she show herself today? Why these two people? Could it be this one-hundredth celebration has roused a spirit?"

Both quickly climb the stairs to see Jason still roaming the room. Behind him stands Celeste, so clear she appears to be alive. Mr. Barkley grabs Victor's arm! The two back quickly out of the room.

"Oh my God, it's real," exclaims Mr. Barkley. "He doesn't appear to see her?"

"I don't think he does," Victor replies. "I watched him when she called him Edward. He didn't respond at all."

Both turn to re-enter the room, but Jason is coming out.

"Jason, this is the owner, Mr. Barkley," Victor explains as they halt him in the doorway. "Do you have a minute to talk about your interests in the tour? We've been asking guests randomly all day what brought them to the open house."

"Sure," Jason responds. "I have always been interested in historical structures. I love the appearance of this place. I had been out riding earlier this spring and found myself here. There were 'No Trespassing' signs up. I told myself if there was ever an open house, I would visit. I'm an architect; the manor lures me in because of its design."

"Okay," Mr. Barkley says with growing interest. He redirects Jason back into the room then proceeds to ask questions of his background. "Do you know anything about the history of the manor?"

"Only what I have read on the Internet and in your brochures," he shares while walking around inspecting the room again. "I think the place has a fascinating history."

"So, no direct history in your past associated with this place? We're interested in finding out if there are any relatives to the Harrington's," Mr. Barkley states.

"No, I'm from this area. I understand they were from New York. I've visited New York, but never lived there."

"Yes, they were originally from New York, but moved to Virginia back in the early 1900s. The family stayed and set up roots here," Mr. Barkley states.

Victor asks, "Would you mind leaving us your contact information? We plan to do a gift drawing for one lucky visitor, and would like to include you."

He hands Victor a card. "Sure, thanks for the tour." He shakes their hands and departs.

Victor glances at the card and reads, "Architect." He finds it fascinating that this guy is an architect, just like Edward. What a coincidence.

"That would explain his presence, but what about Celeste?" Mr. Barkley thinks aloud. "Why did Celeste call him Edward? And why did she show herself with your nine o'clock appointment?"

"I think we need to investigate this further. She did look identical to Celeste," Victor conveys with conviction. "She looked very much like her."

Mr. Barkley tells Victor that he would like to meet her. "Arrange another visit for her when I'm present. I want us to get as much information as we can on both. This is challenging my belief system. I'm an old man seeking answers about life after death, this intrigues me. If there is a connection between Celeste and one of these two, I want to know what it is. Hopefully, the two of them will be interested in learning more as well."

The next day, Victor makes the call to Bridgette. She's surprised to hear from him only a day after the visit.

"Hello," she replies with surprise in her voice. "Yes, I visited the manor yesterday."

Victor says, "You may think this is strange, but the owner of the manor would like to meet you. We had a gift drawing and you are a winner."

Feeling excited about being selected, she responds, "How nice. When would you like me to come pick it up?"

"We have one other guest who has been selected as well, so we need to get with that person first to get his schedule. Is there a particular time that would work best for you?"

"I'm out of school all week, so I'm pretty much available any day," all the while thinking she will cancel anything in conflict with his request.

Victor tells her that he will get back to her once he can set the date. She thanks him, and they hang up.

CHAPTER 3

THE CONTACT

Bridgette receives the return telephone call from Victor within the hour. Victor asks, "Are you available to come to Celestial Manor tomorrow at noon?" Excitedly, she answers yes, happy this is happening so soon. She's unable to get to sleep that night, tossing and turning. She restlessly lays there thinking about her visit. She has read everything imaginable about the property, immersing herself in the details. She didn't know much about her great, great grandmother, as her mother had passed very early in Bridgette's childhood. She ponders the love story between Celeste and Edward. It makes her dreamy, longing for such a love.

She eventually falls into a deep sleep. She dreams she is Celeste, standing at the top of the stairs. Edward is climbing the steps toward her. She is so excited that her heart is pounding as he moves closer. "This doesn't feel like a dream!" she thinks as he continues to climb the steps. She holds out her hand to him and she is surprised when he reaches her and places his hand in hers. She knows she's going to wake up when she feels his hand, but she doesn't. He says nothing as he gazes into her eyes, making her breathless with excitement. As he lowers his head to hers, she gazes into those beautiful blue eyes and thinks of how much she loves them. His hair is jet black, yet his eyes are a sky blue. The contrast between the darkness of his hair and skin against his bright-blue eyes is a compelling combination. The desire in her erupts even before his lips touch hers. His lips press against hers, and she melts into his arms with such longing, a desire she's known from long ago. She returns his kisses with fierce abandon. She struggles to know her true self as she kisses him deeply, placing her fingers behind his neck and pulling him down to her as he envelops her and runs his fingers over her back. Their eyes meet between kisses only to reunite with deeper kisses. The heat from the two ignites a rage of passion that both know will be satisfied this very night.

She is suddenly jolted awake by her alarm beckoning her from a moment that she cannot return to. Devastated, she lies in bed remembering the dream vividly. It felt so real, she thinks to herself as she pushes her body to get up. She falls back onto the bed with anxiety from the let-down of feeling his love so intensely. She repeats in her mind again, and again, the memory of the dream, not wanting to forget a moment of it. "He didn't call me Celeste, and he didn't call me Bridgette either," she thought. She begins doubting what she has dreamed. She has seen pictures of Celeste and Edward, so was it the two of them that she dreamed of, or was it her and someone else? "Maybe it's just me wishing I had the kind of love my great, great grandparents enjoyed." She continues to lie in bed wishing she could sleep again so the dream might begin where it left off.

Frustrated, she forces herself to get up, to prepare for the day's event. Going back to the manor may make her feel the romance again. A new dream could develop or the old one could pick up where it left off, she thinks with great hope. She dresses and begins the drive to Celestial Manor, excited to see the prize she has won.

Pulling into the long stretching road again, she looks at the picturesque manor. This time there are three vehicles in the drive. She feels an eerie sense of belonging to this place as she parks. She searches for the woman in the window that she had seen before, but sees no one. She continues to the front door to go in. Not certain whether she should knock, she hesitates for a moment. The door opens, and Victor is there to meet her.

"Hello, Bridgette," Victor smiles warmly. "So glad you could make it."

"Thank you, Victor."

"Everyone is here," he says as he directs her toward the dining area. As she enters, an older gentleman and a man, who appears to be about 30, are seated at the large table in the dining room, both stand as she walks in.

"Hello, Bridgette," Mr. Barkley says standing and introducing himself. He turns motioning to the other man, "This is Jason Cranston."

Bridgette shakes their hands as Victor pulls out a chair for her to be seated. The table is decorated with place settings for four. She seats herself beside Victor and across from Mr. Barkley. She finds she is nervous with this formal setting, and scolds herself for her casual look, but then notices no one else looks overly dressed either.

Mr. Barkley begins. "I've hired a catering service to provide our lunch." He motions for the caterers to bring in the food to be placed before them. "We can relax and get to know each other. You were selected randomly, as you know, so tell me about yourselves."

Everyone is looking at Bridgette. She begins by telling them she has been in this area her whole life. "My last name is Chandler. My father is a doctor at a local University Hospital. I am an only child. My mother died when she was forty. I was very young at her passing and have few memories of her. I'm in law school and will graduate in six weeks."

Bridgette, Victor, and Mr. Barkley turn to Jason so he starts, "I'm an Architect." He points around the room, "I guess that tells you why I came here for the tour. The structures and the history of beautiful homes intrigue me. I am from a long line of architects, my father was one, as was my grandfather. I, too, have been in this area my whole life. I have a brother a year older than myself, and a sister a year younger."

Bridgette watches him closely. He is well-educated; she can tell by the way he tailors his words. He doesn't have the southern accent that some Virginians have. He is tall, dark, and handsome. As he speaks, she finds herself startled to notice his sky blue eyes. Her mind moves to her dream. No way, she thinks to herself, blushing at the details of the dream. He resembles the man on the steps. They favor each other she admits. Is this the man in my dream? I think I should know, the dark hair and skin, and the eyes are a solid match. Is it him? She's not sure.

Jason sits taking in his situation. The girl or woman across from him is stunning. She has long thick hair that cascades in layers down her back. The brown color has auburn highlights streaking through the strands. Her eyes are a gray blue. They appear gray at first glance, with a hint of blue, which matches perfectly with her olive skin tone and hair color. Her lips are full with a luscious shade of deep natural lipstick emphasizing the plumpness. Her facial features are flawlessly proportioned. She is slender, but her breasts are full, emphasizing the slimness of her waist which he noticed as she entered the room earlier. With no ring on her finger, he makes the assumption she's single. He tries to bring his mind back to the conversation by focusing on Victor, who has just stopped speaking. "Mr. Barkley, Victor, what is this all about? Why were we chosen for this special lunch?" Jason asks with curiosity. "Thank you, by the way."

Victor explains how they were selected for the prizes, but allows Mr. Barkley to provide the details.

"Well, I'm going to be honest with you," Mr. Barkley says handing each an envelope. "First, let me give each of you a five-hundred dollar gift card in honor of being selected. You were chosen not by random drawing, but by incidents that occurred during your visit. The other day when the two of you visited, did either of you have an experience in this house?"

"What kind of experience do you mean?" Jason questions.

Victor asks, "Bridgette, didn't you say you heard someone say, 'Glad you are finally here?'"

"Yes, but I thought you said you didn't hear it?"

"I didn't, but what I did see was Celeste standing behind you at the top of the stairs, right before we left for the tour of the grounds."

"You what?" she says shocked.

"Yes," Victor replies, "she was standing behind you on the staircase."

"Wow! That scares me. What about Jason? What happened with him?"

Jason adds, "Yes, what does this have to do with me?"

"Well, I also saw her in the master suite with you Jason," Victor shares.

Jason and Bridgette just stare at each other pondering their connection to the ghost.

Mr. Barkley begins by telling them the history of the house. Others have known there is a ghost or spirit of Celeste in the house. Some have felt her presence but, until now, no one has actually witnessed her. "The two of you are the only guests causing her to show herself. We would like to walk the premises with you, with your permission, to see if she shows herself again. There's something about the two of you that may be initiating a response from her. She saw you separately, and it provoked her to speak and to appear to us. What will she do if she sees you together? I apologize for bringing you here under false pretenses, and the blunt delivery, but I was afraid you wouldn't come if I told you the truth."

Bridgette sits there pondering whether she should tell them Celeste was her great, great grandmother. She decides to keep it to herself for the moment. She looks at Jason, and he looks back at her with questioning eyes.

Victor sees their concern, "Let's finish lunch, and we'll decide afterwards."

Mr. Barkley changes the subject and offers information about his own life. Why he wants to sell, and how long he has owned the property. "Victor has been my business partner and right-hand man and the handler of this property. It's well past the time to get my things in order since I'm approaching seventy-five. I'll be retiring soon and plan to move abroad once I complete the dissolution of my investments. Victor has been faithful all these years and has stood by me as a business partner through many years. Our business acumen has made both of us financially successful." Changing the subject he comments, "You two youngsters have made a great start on your future, an architect and a lawyer," he smiles. "Do you plan to stay in the area?"

Jason replies, "I do. I have a successful practice here, and I love the area."

Bridgette follows with, "I'd like to stay if I get an offer once I graduate, if not I'll move. I currently have a pre-offer in the area, but I haven't accepted it yet."

"Good for you. I started my professional life about your age, and I planned wisely. It sounds like the two of you are making great plans," Mr. Barkley says. "Well, I hate to change the subject, but will you two agree to go on the tour?"

Bridgette and Jason look at each other, and both nod yes. The four rise from the table and begin the tour making casual conversation as they walk through. Along the way, Jason remarks about the architecture of certain structures and how much it cost to get the marble back in the early 1900's.

As they approach the window with Celeste on it, Jason finds himself examining the portrait then observing Bridgette. "You look like her," he continues looking from her, then back to the image.

Understanding the resemblance, she replies, "Do you think so?"

Victor states, "I thought so the minute I saw you standing next to the window. Bridgette, Chandler is your father's name, what is your mother's maiden name?"

Knowing she could not keep the secret any longer she shares, "As mentioned earlier, my mother died very young, only forty. Her maiden name was Turner. My mother was Catherine's granddaughter. I'm Celeste's great, great granddaughter."

Victor responds, "The resemblance is uncanny. I knew there had to be a relation there. Why didn't you tell us?"

I wanted to hear all about my family without the influence of knowing I was their great, great grandchild."

"This explains it. You look like her. She knew who you were when you came yesterday for your visit," Victor says.

"What about me?" Jason inquires. "Where do I fit into this puzzle?"

"You are exactly that, a puzzle," states Mr. Barkley. "We don't know why Celeste was so captivated with you."

Bridgette thinks to herself, "I do. He's a handsome devil." She smiles internally understanding Celeste's draw to him.

As they turn toward the second set of steps, they see a shadow moving away. Pausing to assess each other, they begin slowly going up the stairway leading to the second floor.

They enter Celeste's room first. Pausing, they wait for something to happen. Each roam into various parts of the room, but watch each other to see if anything is happening.

Soon they hear, "Edward. She is here now. It's time for you to come home."

Everyone stops, stunned and frightened.

Bridgette loses composure and runs to Victor grabbing his arm. Celeste shows herself standing in front of Jason begging him to come to her. Jason looks into her eyes and sees so much pain there. He feels helpless as he stands there unable to respond.

Mr. Barkley breaks the moment by saying, "Okay, let's go."

With this, Celeste disappears. The four leave the room, and walk down the stairs quickly. Once outside, a decision is made to meet again to discuss today's events. Each person leaves with different thoughts of what has just occurred. Mr. Barkley realizes the manor will not sell with a ghost, but is fascinated by the connections the two visitors have to the mansion. Victor decides he will never go there at night. Jason thinks he is a target, but for what reason? He knows nothing about the previous owner. Why does the ghost wish to communicate with him? Bridgette ponders the resemblance she has with the ghost, her great, great grandmother, and why Celeste has chosen Jason to make contact with, as well as her?

All will think twice before returning.

CHAPTER 4

THE HISTORY

Jason leaves unable to rid himself of the image of Celeste. She resembles Bridgette so much. The only difference is the type of curl in their hair. Celeste has cascades of curls, while Bridgette's hair is long and heavy, releasing the curl from tight to loose. Celeste looked at me as if she knew me, but I know nothing about her or Edward. He decides to do some investigation of the family on his own.

He soon finds the births and deaths of both Edward and Celeste on the internet. Edward died suddenly from heart failure in 1922. Celeste soon follows his death a year later. There was speculation that she mourned herself to death. She gave up living when he died. The picture of Edward provides him an understanding why Celeste thought he was Edward. There are similarities he thinks. They had one child, a daughter who married and moved away. Most pictures of Celeste display her hair up in a bun under hats, a common style for the time period. Jason finds it interesting that the portrait of her in the glass is with her hair down, which was revealing. She was beautiful, he decides, as he views a picture of the window in the article he is reading. He feels drawn to her, but he's not sure if it is due to what happened in her room or just getting to know her from his reading. An article describes her as very intelligent and involved in many causes for the less fortunate. The many pictures show large gatherings at Celestial Manor and their New York home, while others are social events. Everyone dressed elegantly and in high fashion.

Jason lies down on his bed thinking about her. As he falls into a light sleep, her face comes into view. He is walking up the steps toward the window. As he gets closer to the top, she appears holding her hand out to him. She says to him, "Edward it is time to come home." Jason is hearing the words, but she is not moving her lips to say it. He climbs to the top of the stairs. He reaches for her hand and finds himself saying, "Soon my love, soon." Suddenly he jumps awake, removing him from the dream. "Whew!" He sits up. He is alarmed by the reality he just felt in the dream. He can't seem to shake her. What did soon mean? Why did he say that? His thoughts are so focused that he feels out of control a bit. He shakes it off and jumps in the shower to get ready for bed. He hopes as he showers that the dream doesn't return, all the while pondering what 'soon' meant.

Bridgette calls her dad the minute she leaves Celestial Manor to ask if she can stop by on her way home. When she arrives, she finds her father in the den reading. "Dad, mom's maiden name was Turner, right? I know nothing about mom's grand-parents, or great grandparents."

Her dad replies, "The Harrington's died long before your mother was born. Your mother knew nothing about them."

Bridgette asks, "Dad, do you know anything about them?"

"Not much. Only that they both were from prominent families. The families originated from New York, and they moved to the area in the early 1900's, when your great, great grandfather brought them to Virginia to live in their summer house."

"Dad, have you ever heard of a place called Celestial Manor?"

"Well, yes, I have. I heard it was some kind of mausoleum that no one wanted a part of. Catherine didn't want to live in that big house and left it empty for years. Your grandfather sold it and put the money in a fund for the future. Your mother and I married young. Your mother was only nineteen when we married. Your great, great grandfather passed when Catherine was only eight years old, then Celeste passed away a year later. Your mother said Celeste didn't take Edward's death well. Why are you asking all of these questions, honey?"

"Dad, I went to visit Celestial Manor this morning wanting to learn more about the history of our family. Do you think I resemble my great, great grandmother?"

"Well I hadn't thought about it. Wait, your mother had some pictures." He left the room to retrieve them. He returns with picture albums and a box of loose pictures. He sorts through many pictures to get to those of Celeste. "There she is." He points to a picture of a lovely woman posing in a long elegant dress, holding a fashionable umbrella on her arm. She has on a large hat, and holds a small purse.

Bridgette asks, "I can't see her face that well because of the hat. Dad, are there any more pictures?"

"Let's see." He flips through more pages then finds a whole section dedicated to Celeste. Some pictures are with her hair down, but many other photos are with her hair in the pulled up style of the day. "You do favor her, Bridgette. I never noticed it before, but you do look a lot like her."

"Dad, I do! May I take some of these pictures? I'll bring them back. I want to show them to the owner of Celestial Manor. They were asking me if I had any family history with the Harrington's. Truthfully, I didn't know any details about my great, great grandmother at all, so I couldn't tell them much. She died years ago, many years before I was born."

"Sure honey, you can take them, but take care of them. They're very old."

"I will, dad. I promise." She begins picking out the pictures that she thinks are applicable to her point. She selects those showing their resemblance. "Thanks dad." She decides not to share the ghost part of her visit, because she knows her dad would demand that she never return to that place again.

Bridgette leaves with pictures in hand. Driving home, she reviews the events of the day. The whole situation confuses her. She is glad she's off for the week to search for more information regarding her family history.

CHAPTER 5

COMPARING CONTACTS

Jason had handed Bridgette his business card as they were leaving Celestial Manor that day. She turns the card repeatedly in her hands, trying to decide whether to contact him. She wants to discuss with him the fact that she is a relative and what his connection could possibly be. She nervously dials his number and waits for him to pick up.

A woman answers the phone, "Hello, Jason Cranston's office."

"Hello, may I speak to Mr. Cranston please? This is Bridgette Chandler calling."

The receptionist tells her to, "Hold, please."

She hears a click, then "Hello. This is Jason."

"Hello, Jason. This is Bridgette Chandler. I met you yesterday at Celestial Manor."

"Hello, Bridgette. How are you?"

"Fine. I have some news I'd like to share with you about Celeste. Do you have time to meet for lunch today?" she asks somewhat pensive.

He says, "Sure, what time and where?"

"I'm off this week, so name a place. Do you want to meet close to your office?" she offers.

"Uh, sure," he says trying to think of a place. "Have you been to the Ivy Inn? That's pretty close."

"Noon sound okay?"

"Sounds great, see you then," he hangs up.

Both arrive at the same time, pulling in beside each other. He casually gets out of his car and walks over to open her car door. The aroma of her perfume reaches him and stimulates his senses to her beauty. Her long hair is glistening from the sun light.

Her face is faultlessly proportioned and beautiful. He takes her hand to help her out of the car. She has on a mid-thigh navy blue skirt with tan platform sandals. Although she is shorter than he is, her legs are very long and tan. The blue and tan silk blouse brings the ensemble together perfectly. He says, "Hello, you look nice."

"Thanks, Jason. This was perfect timing, arriving at the same time. I appreciate you meeting me on such short notice," she remarks as she clicks the remote to lock the car door. He clicks his as well. She turns toward him taking in his handsome features. "He is hot," she thinks to herself. Dressed in a white shirt and black tie, he is the epitome of a perfect man. His strong jaw line, short dark hair, and those beautiful blue eyes captivate her. Embarrassed, she is obviously gaping, she is relieved when he continues the conversation as if he doesn't notice.

"You have me intrigued since you called so soon after our meeting."

They enter the restaurant, and the host seats them without any waiting. The waiter approaches to take their drink order. Both reply with their drink preference of un-sweetened tea, then order the salad buffet before the waiter leaves.

"After I left Celestial Manor yesterday," Bridgette begins, "I went to my father's house to ask some questions about my family. I have never heard any history about my great, great grandmother and grandfather, so I was curious after yesterday's revelations."

He conveys, "I knew you were related before you told us. You look too much like her not to be."

As she pulls the pictures out of her purse, she agrees, "I know, I can't believe how much I resemble her. Look, we found these pictures of her in our family album."

He takes the pictures and goes through them one by one, comparing Bridgette and Celeste. "Wow, you really are a dead ringer; there is no denying it in these pictures. Sorry for the dead ringer," he smiles.

"It excites me Jason! I have never known much about mother's family history. I didn't know anything past the life of my mother truthfully. I know dad's family, but not mom's. With mom dying when I was so young, I am more aware of dad's side of the family. Seeing these pictures, it's as if I am in Celeste's image. I look more like Celeste than I do my own mother. Do you have any idea why Celeste has attached herself to you?"

"No, I haven't a clue." He ponders the statement aloud, "'It's time to come home, Edward'. She has to be confusing me for him."

"That's what I think too," Bridgette states. "Do you believe in reincarnation?"

He replies, "I haven't thought about it. Until now, I have never considered ghosts, much less something as deep as reincarnation."

She questions him, "What are we going to do about it?"

"What do you mean? What can we do?" he asks wondering where she was going with this.

"I think we need to ask her. Have you heard of those who go into homes to discover if there are ghosts and try to contact them?"

"Yes, but I don't know of anyone in this area, do you?"

"No," but I did find a web page on the internet that says they can connect you to a Paranormal Society anywhere in the United States." She tells him, "I think we should at least try to find out what Celeste wants with us, don't you? I want her to find peace. It's like she's stuck here seeking Edward. She thinks you are Edward. Maybe we can help her move on."

"I guess so, but I'm not comfortable with this ghost stuff."

"Neither am I," she hesitates, "but I'm willing if you are."

"Let me think about it," Jason says not able to devise an excuse to get out of it.

"It's you she wants, Jason. If you don't help her, I don't think she can move on."

"Just let me think about it, Okay?"

"Sure, I'm sorry. I'm so wrapped up in this. I do understand your hesitation. I'm sure you would want to consider this seriously; before agreeing to help, but it's personal for me."

Jason responds, "I will seriously think about it, Bridgette. How soon are you thinking about starting this?"

"I'm ready to seek out someone who deals with ghosts. You think about things, and when you've made a decision, give me a call. If I don't hear from you, I'll begin without you. I'm certain

Victor and Mr. Barkley will show interest. I just don't want to do this alone. I won't have hard feelings if you decide you want no part of it."

"Good. Thanks, I appreciate that. I'll think it over."

The two spend the rest of lunch talking about their lives, getting to know each other as Bridgette and Jason.

After a few days, Bridgette contacts the local Paranormal Society to discover the process for communicating with ghosts. She is told that if she has already seen the ghost, the ghost wants to communicate with her and has a message for her. Bridgette is advised to go back and tell Celeste she wants to help her. Someone from the Paranormal Society would be willing to attend the contact event. She agrees that she wants that, and would be in touch regarding the date. First, Bridgette wants to study the history of Celeste and Edward. She gathers everything she can find about them. She researches their lives in New York, as well as the years they spent here locally. The love story is full of warmth and affection from two souls who unite in a marriage of commitment and respect. After hours of reading about the couple, Bridgette sets down her laptop to find she's exhausted. She showers and climbs into bed. She dreams that night of Celeste. "Come to me Bridgette," was the message repeated over and over in her dreams. The next morning she decides to go back to the manor alone to see if Celeste will contact her.

The manor is open for tours from 11:00 a.m. until 5:00 p.m. As she walks in, she is asked if she wants the historical guide or an independent tour. "I want to go alone, thank you." She heads up the steps leading directly to Celeste and Edward's master suite. Outside of each door stands an attendant. She smiles at the attendant and timidly enters, watching for any sign of Celeste's presence. When she sees no one, relief fills her because she's afraid. At the same time, she is also disappointed that Celeste is not here. She begins walking casually around the room looking at all the delicate trinkets. She picks up a hairbrush made of tinted pink glass. She pulls a string of Celeste's hair from it and lays the brush back down. Without warning, the door slams shut. Bridgette turns quickly around to see Celeste standing across the room from her.

She waits for Celeste to say something, but Celeste stands in silence.

Bridgette, visibly shaking with fear speaks, "Celeste, I have come to help you."

"Be not afraid my dear child," Celeste finally communicates. "I'll not harm you. I have been waiting for you."

"Why?" Bridgette says in confusion. "How can I help you?"

"Edward will come to me now that you are here."

"What does my being here have to do with Edward coming to you? How am I able to help?"

"You will see, my dear." As Celeste finishes these words, she rushes toward Bridgette, who immediately collapses from fear.

The door suddenly opens. The attendant rushes in to find Bridgette unconscious on the floor. The attendant runs screaming down the hall for help. Bridgette is taken by ambulance to the hospital where her father is on duty. The attending physician in the emergency-room summons her father informing him of his daughter's admittance. Her father is told her condition can't be explained. Her vitals and brain scans show normal. We have no explanation for her unconscious state.

Bridgette knows why. In her deep state of unconsciousness, Celeste is taking Bridgette on a journey of love, showing her the lives of Celeste and Edward, through the eyes and heart of Celeste.

CHAPTER 6

CELESTE'S REVEAL

YEAR 1910

In Bridgette's comatose state, she is taken by Celeste, mind, body and soul, to reveal the love story she shares with Edward. She becomes a part of two worlds, two hearts, one home.

BRIDGETTE BECOMES CELESTE

As Celeste walks through the park near the waters, she inhales deeply, filling her senses with the sweet smell of flowers. The grass is a vivid green, stately manicured for hosting the wealthy. She's walking the grounds of a private club in New York where socialites gather to drink tea and chatter about current events. She's not in the mood today to chat with women. She wants to be alone. Strolling with an umbrella in hand, she guards her delicate skin against the harsh rays from the sun. Her olive complexion needs no sun to caress it. The gown she wears is pale blue. The bodice is gathered under her breasts fitting tightly all the way to her waist with a sash that separates the bodice from the skirt. Embroidery cascades over the material and down a small train on the back. The bust of the dress has a rounded neckline with a respectable view of her assets. She feels full of joy today, smiling while casually twirling her umbrella. She sees her reflection as she passes by the water's edge. She looks away, and then glances back at her reflection. She sees another reflection close behind hers. Determined not to let this person know she sees him, she takes an abrupt turn. She moves away from the water's edge to find he has sidestepped in front of her.

Tipping his hat to her he excuses himself, "Madam, please, accept my apologies."

"That's quite all right," she says bringing her umbrella down, closing it beside her. "Did I strike you with my umbrella?"

"No, but thank you for asking," He politely continues while removing his hat, "Let me introduce myself. My name is Edward. I've been watching you from the window." He points to the main club area. "May I be so bold as to ask your name?"

Celeste looks at this handsome man, and then back up to the club window, smiles, and replies, "My name is Celeste, Celeste Morgan."

"Ah, he says thoughtfully. Are you related to the Morgan's from Manhattan?"

"Yes, my father is William Morgan," she looks a little surprised that he may know her father.

"I have met your father, Ms. Morgan. He and I travel in the same circles. We are both architects. Our paths have crossed on many occasions. I just saw him inside. That's how I made the connection. Is this the first time you have accompanied your father?"

"No, I am here often. Have you been less attentive to have missed me Mr.?" she smiles teasing him.

"Harrington," he smiles. "Have you noticed me here before, Ms. Morgan?"

"No, I have not Mr. Harrington," she grins, turning her face away to smile.

"Then we are both guilty of an inexcusable act," he announces playfully. "Our days would have been much happier if we had met earlier, don't you agree Ms. Morgan?"

Turning to walk toward the club she decides, "I will hold that decision until I know you better."

"I will take that as an invitation to dinner," he responds expertly catching up to her as she heads back.

"I don't invite men to dinner," she says modestly.

"But of course, Ms. Morgan. May I have the pleasure of your company in the dining hall tonight?"

She stops, turning to gaze directly at him analyzing his face. He has enticing blue eyes, she thinks to herself. "You may," she says as she sees her father waiting for her on the terrace. "I will meet you in the dining hall, at say, seven?" She leaves him before getting an answer, and moves quickly toward her father.

"Seven is perfect," he yells after her.

She reaches her father and kisses him on the cheek.

Her father waves at Edward and questions her, "Celeste, I didn't know you knew Edward Harrington?"

"I don't father. We just met while walking the lawn. He has asked me to join him for dinner tonight. Is that acceptable to you?"

"Yes. He's a fine young man. I don't see a problem with that at all." Her father takes a second look at Edward as if deciding whether it is truly a good idea. He is surprised that Celeste has accepted the dinner invitation so quickly. That's certainly not like her.

At seven, Celeste walks into the main dining hall where Edward is waiting. Edward spots her as she enters, and walks slowly toward her, taking in all her beauty. "You take my breath away, Ms. Morgan." He reaches for her hand telling her how lovely she is. She is dressed in a couture evening gown, with a corseted waist and a full crinoline skirt. The gown is emerald green, with ornamented white designs.

She gives a slight curtsy, "Thank you, Mr. Harrington. You look dashing and very handsome." He is wearing a back suite with a crisp white shirt and black tie.

The host approaches Edward and says, "Your table is ready, sir."

Edward places her arm in his, leading her to the dining hall. He decides this is a perfect start to a beautiful evening.

By night's end, Celeste feels she has known this man all her life. He is humorous, quick-witted, and makes her feel like a queen without any words spoken. His blue eyes tell of his affections, at times making her flush with excitement. For the first time in her young life, she has met someone who doesn't bore her. She has had many suitors vying for her affections, but she has never felt the least bit interested. It's been challenging listening to men go on and on about her. Edward is different. He has only to glance at her to create excitement. She knows in her heart, that he is the one.

The next few weeks are filled with laughter and wonderful moments. Edward speaks with Celeste's father to request permission to escort her on outings. Mr. Morgan agrees, asking him to respect his daughter at all times. Edward happily agrees to those terms and begins making plans. They go on buggy rides around New York, the theater, and a ball given in honor of the city's leaders. Her father is there at the ball and watches his daughter with great satisfaction. She looks as if she is having the time of her life.

Celeste dances until her feet are swollen.

Edward revels in this delightful girl who in only a month has changed his life. The orchestra plays a soft melodic song that provides him the opportunity to speak his feelings to her.

"Celeste, you have captured my heart."

She looks up into his blue eyes and becomes lost in them. "I feel the same for you, Edward."

He whispers in her ear that he cannot live without her. "I know we have just met, but I have never felt this way before. I know my heart, and you are the one for me." He releases her, then takes her hand and pulls her through the crowd, going out onto the balcony. He turns her around and kisses her with great demand. Her lips meet his with the same frenzy. They caress each other with warm deep kisses that shake her to the core. He feels dizzy with lust for her. "I need you, Celeste," he moans in a deep husky voice.

Realizing she is losing control of the situation, she pulls away from him. "Edward, it is far too soon to speak or embrace as we just did." She surveys the area to see if anyone had witnessed what had occurred. She looks back into his eyes and touches his chiseled face with her fingers. "I have fallen for you, but we must make sure this is right for us. There is much to consider. My family is leaving New York soon to move to Virginia, so I am leaving. This has been wonderful, but we are two shadows passing through the night, and we must wake up from our dream." She pulls away from him and walks back into the ballroom. Her father spots her right away and sees the distress on his daughter's face.

He makes his way to her and reaches her just as Edward walks up behind her.

"Is everything okay, Celeste?" her father asks with concern as his wife walks up behind him.

Edward steps forward and says to Mr. and Mrs. Morgan. "I have just spoken words of love to Celeste, and I think it took her by surprise. It has surprised me as well, Mr. Morgan, but I have fallen in love with your daughter. I know it has been a short amount of time, but I know my heart, and it belongs to her."

Mr. Morgan observes his daughter to gauge her feelings.

"Father, I feel the same, but it's too soon."

Mr. Morgan looks at Elizabeth, Celeste's mother, then back at Edward and says, "Edward, Celeste's mother and I thank you for your honesty, but now I think it is time that we take Celeste home. We can pick this conversation up at a later time when appropriate. Please feel free to call on us say, midday tomorrow?"

"Sir, of course. I understand, but I brought her; I will gladly see her home safely."

"Thank you, Edward, but Celeste, her mother, and I need some time to talk. I think our ride home will provide us that opportunity. Please say good night, Celeste."

She sees the disappointed Edward. She kisses him on the cheek, then turns to depart with her father and mother, leaving Edward to stare after them.

Celeste's father speaks to her on their drive home about the love he has for her mother. The comparisons are the same he tells her. "I fell deeply for your mother. She was the most beautiful woman I had ever laid my eyes on." She sees her mother reach over and squeeze her father's hand. "I like Edward. He is a respected man in the city. I don't encourage a quick decision, but if a quick decision is to occur, I want you to know that I fell for your mother just as quickly."

"Father, what about our family leaving New York? I won't live here without you. I would never see him if we leave."

"Honey, if you decide to be with Edward, your life is here. I know the thought of leaving you behind will be difficult for us, but eventually I would be giving you over to your husband anyway. Do you think you are ready for marriage?"

"Father, he hasn't asked me to marry him. He only spoke words of love, not marriage."

"Honey, I am certain, when he arrives tomorrow, he will ask for your hand in marriage. I need to know what answer to give him. Is Edward someone you could see your life with?"

"I think so father, but I am not sure about marriage."

"You will know when it is right my sweet girl. You will know.

CHAPTER 7

THE DECISION

The next morning Celeste rises early. She dresses and walks down to breakfast. Her father and mother are already seated at the breakfast table. He passes her the juice, and points to the buffet. "I had the staff prepare a platter for us. I couldn't decide what I wanted, so I had them fix a little of everything."

"Thank you, father. I'll eat a little, but I'm not very hungry this morning. The wine from last night has given me a bit of a headache."

"I had a small headache myself this morning. Eat something, you'll feel better," he says kissing her on her cheek as she gets up to go to the buffet. "Your mother and I have news for you this morning. My offer on the estate in Virginia has been accepted."

"It's decided then? We are moving to Virginia?" she asks feeling the turmoil of last night rising again.

"Yes, we made the final decision this morning. We're moving. I'm ready to retire, honey. I want the laid-back life I found in Virginia."

"Father, this is terrible timing," tears well up in her eyes.

Her mother tells her that a decision doesn't have to be made now about Edward, if she's not ready. "Maybe a separation is what the two of you need. You need time to find out how you feel about one another."

"I don't want to leave him or you. I don't want it to be one way or the other," she feels defeated. Celeste finishes her meal, deciding to take a walk. She grabs her umbrella on the way out the door. Leaving the brownstone, she walks down the street to the small park. She finds a nice spot to be alone. She lowers her umbrella raising her face to the sky. Her hair is half up, half down, and pulled to the back of her head. The sun is warm on her exposed face. She closes her eyes and tries to imagine her life without her parents, or a life without Edward. Neither makes sense. What started as a flourishing relationship is now turning into a decision she's not ready to make.

After an hour she returns to the brownstone with decisiveness. She will leave along with her parents. It's too soon to make wedding decisions. She thinks her father is exaggerating Edward's possible proposal anyway. She feels relieved with her decision, but entering the hallway, she hears Edward's voice. She returns to the puddle of confusion. Her heart leaps at the mere sound of his voice. She walks into the Gentlemen's quarters where both are seated laughing freely. As she enters, Edward and her father stand to allow her to be seated.

"Good afternoon, Celeste. You are looking lovely today."

"Good afternoon, Edward. Thank you."

Everyone sits and Edward states, "I have just finished speaking to your father about my feelings for you. I have stated clearly that I want his blessing for us to wed. He feels we need to discuss this further before he gives his blessing."

"You asked for my hand in marriage?"

"Of course," he replies with an expressive look that she should have known.

"I mean, I know we have feelings for one another, but marriage?"

Her father clears his throat and stands. "I will leave the two of you to discuss this on your own. I will be in the study if you need me." He pats her hand as he leaves.

Edward begins right away. "Celeste, you don't share the same feelings as I do?"

"Yes, but marriage? So soon?"

"Your father explained fully your dilemma about them leaving New York, and your misgivings about it."

"Well yes, for my parents to leave without me would be devastating."

"I will take you to see them whenever you want," he says with great promise.

"I know you would, but I couldn't be that far from them. I'm sorry, Edward, but my answer has to be no."

He stares in disbelief. Rubbing his hand through his hair, he says, "Celeste, please think this through. Don't make a rash decision."

"Of course, I'm not! I feel the same way you do, but I can't let my parents leave without me."

He stands, holding his hat in his hand. "I'm sorry you feel this way." With devastation on his face, he turns and leaves.

Celeste breaks down in tears and runs to her room. She falls onto the bed sobbing. She has just let the man of her dreams go. How will she ever live with that?

She remains to herself in a state of immense pain at the loss of Edward for the next few days. She attends meals with the family, sitting in silence. Her parents are talking about the plans for Virginia with great excitement. She thinks to herself, "How can they be so selfish? It's as if they don't know that my heart is broken."

After three days of letting his daughter sulk, her father knocks on the door of her room. "May I come in, Celeste?"

"Come in, father," she says with a pitifully sad voice.

He walks in leaving the door half open. He sits in the big chair in front of the fireplace. Celeste is sitting on her bed. "Come sit near me, honey." She gets off of the bed, and moves to the chair in front of him.

"Celeste, you cannot keep going on like this any longer. You have made your choice not to marry him. If that is not the correct decision for you, then tell him, but you cannot live in this mourning state of existence forever."

"I know, father, but I'm hurting. I care for him. Knowing he loves me too makes it harder for me to let go."

"Then maybe you haven't made the correct decision."

She sits in silence pondering his words. She looks up at her father as tears roll from her eyes. "It's too late now father. I have already turned him down."

"Are you saying you have changed your mind, Celeste? He is a very nice young man whom I think would make you a good husband."

"I have changed my mind, father."

"That's what I thought. Edward, come on in!"

She jumps from the chair in shock. "Edward, what are you doing here?"

"Your father called to tell me how unhappy you are. Maybe we should talk and revisit the proposal," he smiles at her.

"Father, I love you so much! How did you know?"

"I think those tears of yours told me all I needed to know." With that, he says, "Come on you two. Go down to the parlor and talk this out. Mother and I will be on the patio if you need us."

Edward grabs Celeste's hand, and they hurry downstairs.

"Celeste, I have found I can't live without you. Marry me!"

"By choosing you, Edward, I will lose my parents. I am very upset about that. They are leaving New York."

"What if I promise to take you to visit often? I will even go so far as to build a summer home for you there. Will that make you stay with me Celeste?"

At that moment, she knows he is meant for her. He is willing to make sacrifices so that she can see her parents. He didn't make her feel terrible about still needing to cling to her family. "I will marry you, Edward. I love you with all my heart!" She jumps in his arms kissing him on the cheek, on the forehead, then finally on his mouth. "Let's go tell mother and father." She grabs his hand and they walk outside to break the news to her parents.

Celeste's mother and father are so happy. Her father shakes Edward's hand and tells him, "Take good care of my daughter, Edward. I trust you with my most valuable possession."

Edward assures him with a nod. "Sir, at this time, I would like to ask formally, for your daughter's hand in marriage."

With emotion muffling his voice, Celeste's father responds, "You have my permission son."

Celeste's mother embraces her daughter, excited with the good news. She turns to Edward, giving him a hug as well. Looking back to Celeste, she exclaims, "We have a wedding to plan!"

"I know, mother. I can't believe it!"

Edward interrupts the conversation. "Celeste, I hate to break up this happy moment, but I would like to go tell my parents. Will that be okay with you, Mr. and Mrs. Morgan?"

"Yes, of course, Edward. You two run along. Edward, call me William. You will soon be family."

"Thank you, sir. I mean, William. Thank you very much." He grabs Celeste's hand, and they rush out the door.

CHAPTER 8

THE WEDDING

Four short weeks later, the pews of the church are packed full of socialites. It's the most talked about wedding of the century. Two well-to-do families are joining through this wonderful union. The bride is a ball of nerves. Celeste and her mother have perfectly planned the wedding. Everything is exactly as it should be. The church is adorned with flowers everywhere. Candelabras placed strategically provide a soft glow throughout the venue. "Nothing could be more breathtaking, mother. Thank you so much for postponing your move to Virginia. I couldn't have made this happen without you."

They hurry off to a corner room to dress for the wedding. She has chosen a white dress that has a high lace collar and sleeves. The silk corseted bodice meets the waist where it tapers to a V. The many layers of silk and lace on the skirt cascade down the rest of the dress to the floor. The skirt falls away from her bottom as it meets the train of ruffles trailing two feet behind her. The style compliments her slim figure by hugging her curves. She grabs her mother's hand while they gaze into the mirror together. "Mother! I feel so special in this dress. I hope Edward loves it as much as I do."

"It's you in the dress my darling that makes it special. You are the most beautiful bride I have ever seen." They hug trying to hold back the tears of joy. Her mother pulls out a set of pearls. "This is your 'something new'." She fastens them around her neck. She hands her a pair of silk white gloves. "I wore these when your father and I married, so this is something borrowed." Next she pulls out a blue garter made of piper lace. "Now you have something blue."

Celeste blushes, "Mother!"

"Today you become a woman, Celeste. It's time you know about grown-up things. It is so important to be attentive to your husband. Never take him for granted just because you are his wife. Always keep his attention, and never give him a reason to wander."

"I understand, mother. I will be the best wife he could want. I promise." Looking in the mirror she says, "I'm so nervous. How will I know what to do on my wedding night?"

"If he is the man I think he is, you will not need to worry. He loves you so much, Celeste. I know he wants to show you how much. It's the natural next step of love between a man and a woman. You will know each other intimately; this will bring you a deeper, more enduring love."

Celeste shares, "I didn't know I could love him more than I already do."

As the wedding march begins, Celeste views the aisle. She sees the man she will be spending the rest of her life with. He is looking at her with so much love, it makes her heart leap up in her throat. She wants to cry with emotion, but holds it together as she passes friends and family in the pews. Her mother, Elizabeth, is on the front row in a designer blue dress holding a kerchief tapping the tears streaming from her eyes. His parents are on the groom's side smiling contentedly at their soon-to-be daughter-in-law. As they approach, her father lays her hand in Edward's.

"Take care of her, Edward."

"I will love her always," Edward says as he takes and squeezes her hand. He observes Celeste and whispers, "You are so beautiful."

The ceremony is a blur for her. The evening gala celebration for the couple is impressive with champagne, rounds and rounds of toast after toast for the happy couple. Her head is spinning from the attention and well wishes. Edward never leaves her side the whole night. It's getting late when Edward looks at her and says, "We should be going."

"Where are we going Edward? You haven't shared the plans with me."

"We are staying the night at the Plaza Hotel. Tomorrow, I have a surprise for you."

She pokes him, "What is it?"

"Tomorrow, my love, tomorrow," then kisses her on her cheek.

They arrive at the hotel pulling up to the front door. The hotel attendees hurry out to grab their bags. "Good evening, Mr. Harrington. Welcome to the Plaza."

"Thank you, my good man. Thank you."

They are escorted to their suite where they see congratulatory flowers are everywhere when they open the door. "Oh, my goodness," she expresses amazed at the wall-to-wall flowers in every corner.

She starts to walk in but Edward stops her, "Wait, I need to carry you over the threshold."

She laughs as he picks her up dramatically twirling her around after entering the doorway. They both laugh openly as he puts her down. Turning to the attendees, he thanks them and places small coins in their hands. "Please put up a do not disturb sign on your way out." They depart with a thank-you, and close the door behind them as they leave. He is quick to lock the door.

Edward walks to Celeste and begins kissing her lightly on the lips. "Hello, Mrs. Harrington."

"Hello, Mr. Harrington."

"Oh no, 'that's husband' to you." He smiles as he carefully kisses her lips again. He takes her face into his hands, pressing his lips firmly on hers with urgent enthusiasm. She has never kissed with this amount of fervor. She wants the heated exchange to go on and on. As it intensifies, she feels a surge of heat come over her. She has never felt this before. She has a fire down in her belly that makes her yearn for him. As Edward says he loves her, she notices his voice is husky and deeper. Getting caught up in the moment she grabs for him as his face is buried in her neck.

Her scent drives him to need her now. He stops himself. Kissing her delicately on the lips he suggests, "Darling, why don't you get yourself comfortable, while I get us drinks?"

She pulls away slowly staring dreamily into his eyes. She turns, grabbing her luggage, but he takes it from her, to carry it to the dressing area in the next room.

He motions toward the luggage, telling her to grab the smaller bag as well.

She turns and picks it up following behind him.

It's a small room, perfect for changing with privacy. As he gets ready to leave, she says, "Edward, will you undo the back of my dress? I'm afraid I can't reach it."

He returns and begins unfastening the buttons on the back of the dress. As each button is unhooked, the dress falls away. Her bare back begins to appear with each unfastened button. When the dress gives way to her bare skin, he reaches down to kiss her in the middle of her back. Her breath catches. She breathes deeply causing her chest to rise and fall.

Edward backs away from her, raises his eyebrows and smiles as he leaves the room. She frantically removes the dress putting on a night gown that is low cut with shear gatherings around the collar. There are small ruffles that drape gently across her breasts showing cleavage meant specifically for a seductive night. It leaves no doubts of its purpose. It flows generously across her body, swaying as she walks. She removes the pins from her hair to let it fall freely down her back. She fluffs it to loosen the curls. Looking into the standing mirror, she feels pleased with her choice for her first night.

Edward is setting up the room for a romantic evening. He changes his attire into a man's robe. He has pajama pants on, but no top. He pulls back the bed covering for preparation. Pouring two glasses of wine, he sits them on the small table in front of the sofa. He surveys the room nervously for anything he may have forgotten.

Celeste opens the door to see him sitting on the sofa with a glass of wine in his hand.

He stands, silenced by her beauty.

She becomes self-conscious as he continues to stare at her. "Edward, stop," she blushes seeing him looking directly at her fully exposed cleavage.

The material is so sheer he is able to see her nipples through the gown. "Celeste, you are above anything I could ever have imagined."

She smiles sheepishly and says nothing.

He says, "Come here, darling." She walks over to him. He pulls her down, seating her beside him on the sofa. He hands her the glass of wine and holds his glass up for a toast. "To the most beautiful woman in the world, who is now my wife. I am the luckiest man alive."

"To my husband, whom I love more than life itself." They click glasses and sip their wine.

Edward watches her and when her glass is empty, he places both on the table. He pulls her close to him. His hand rubs along her jaw line pushing her hair back behind her ear. His lips press sweetly on hers with a non-demanding peck, a nibble. He parts her lips for a deeper kiss, searching with pressing vigor. She is overwhelmed with this new Edward and feels uncertain of what to do. Parting her lips for him, she gives in to his probing tongue. Slowly, she begins returning his kisses with as much abandon as his.

Between kisses he muffles, "I love you."

She says, "I love you, too." Her heart is pounding as she anticipates the unknown. He stands and picks her up, carrying her to the bed. They sit side by side as he begins kissing her again and again, moving down her throat to the soft mound of her breasts. She gasps, breathless from his probing lips on her bare skin. His lips feel hot moving skillfully over her body. The depth of passion is new to her, so she follows his lead.

As he discovers his bride, he softly touches her hair, pushing it from her face. "You are everything I have ever wanted, Celeste."

She grabs onto him whispering words of love repeating his name over and over, "Edward, Edward." She moans deep in her throat as he intensifies his demands on her then ultimately penetrates the forbidden place. She moans with pain as he breaches her mark of virginity.

He stops and apologizes. "I'm sorry, Celeste."

"I didn't know it would hurt so much," she says holding still for a moment.

He kisses her sweetly, then continues slowly. Taking his time he discovers every part of her bringing her beyond the pain to learn what true passion is. As their love climaxes with ecstasy, he gives a deep groan, satisfaction radiating through his whole body.

She feels herself letting go, and finds she is in a state of spasmodic convulsions that sends pleasure throughout her whole body.

He is breathless as he collapses on top of her spent with love. Depleted, both lay breathing heavily. Bringing her to his side, he kisses her warmly and asks, "Are you Okay?"

"Yes."

"You're quiet. Did I hurt you?"

"I never knew love making was like this. It's so personal."

"Yes, it is," he kisses her sweetly on the lips pulling her in closer to snuggle. Both lay satisfied with their first night of consummating their marriage. He unconsciously rubs her arm with his hand. Eventually slowing the motion, he begins breathing heavily into her hair, signifying he has fallen asleep.

She lay there thinking about what just happened with him. She never knew it was like this, so revealing with such abandonment. That night they made love several more times before dawn. As she dozes off after their last passionate love making, she thinks, "Life is wonderful!"

The next morning they go downstairs to the dining hall for breakfast. Celeste feels as if everyone is staring at her. "Do they know what we have been doing, Edward?"

His smile widens as he reaches to kiss her lightly on the lips. "I suspect they have been doing the very same thing darling," he whispers with humor in his words.

She examines the room. In fact, no one is looking at her. She relaxes a little from her paranoia and enjoys her breakfast. "I have worked up an appetite."

With a big grin spread across his face, he declares, "We both did, darling. Are you ready for your surprise?" he asks.

"Yes, what is it?"

"In two hours, we will be boarding a ship bound for Italy."

"What? Edward, are you teasing?! Really?"

"I knew you'd be happy. We will be spending our honeymoon at *Almona Deltara*, an Italian Manor in Tuscany."

In two hours, they are standing on the deck of a large ship headed for Italy. It's a dream come true. She had been abroad with her family, but never to Italy. She holds on to her husband's arm standing on the deck waving good-bye to her family. They escorted them to board their ship. As the ship moves further out to sea, the city gets smaller and smaller, eventually disappearing from view.

They spend two glorious weeks on the ship, walking decks, and sharing wonderful evenings full of dining and dancing. She gets to know the lighter side of Edward. They laugh non-stop. Enjoying the entertainment provided by the ship, they have whirlwind evenings only to culminate in passionate love making each night. They are seated at the Captain's table during dinner, but choose on many nights to dine in their quarters. Intimate nights of love making are chosen over the commotion of the ship and the evening galas.

Arriving at the *Almona Deltara*, they unpack and lazily walk the vineyard fields. The rolling hills are lush and green stretching for miles. They do absolutely nothing but share their thoughts and take time getting to know one another. The two weeks are spent only with each other. Their love grows beyond belief. She trusts this man implicitly with her heart.

He loves her more and more each day. Their brief time together has grown into a union of marital bliss and companionship that they are blessed to find.

CHAPTER 9

RETURN WITH NO PARENTS

The trip home is bittersweet. It's time to begin a new life with her gorgeous husband. She watches him as he concentrates on pressing matters. Sitting at a small table in the corner of their room on the ship, he pulls out papers. He's getting back to business. She can see by the serious focus on the paper he reads. An appearance she hasn't seen since before their wedding day. She pours a glass of tea. Holding it out to him, she smiles. He lays the papers down taking her free hand and kissing it with his lips. Taking the glass, he drinks and sighs with pleasure.

"I needed this. How did I get so lucky?"

"You are very lucky," she displays a teasing grin.

"Oh, I agree with that." He sets the glass on the table, and jumps up to grab her. She sees the playfulness in his face and backs away to escape his mischievous attempts to take her.

He is so attracted to her. He can't think of doing anything other than making love to her. He chases, and catches her, backing her into the wall as he turns her around to devour her. Taking her with fevered kisses, he buries his head in the curve of her neck. The sweet smell of rose water lingers on her skin. He demands teasing, "How can I get work done with you around? My business will collapse. You torture me with your presence. I can't focus on anything but you."

She looks into those blue eyes and sees the love in them. "I love you, Edward. I'm so glad I married you."

He brings his face even with hers. He stares into those eyes, with long, thick lashes. The gray blue eyes captivate him. Her smooth skin is flawless. "God you are beautiful," he stares at her. Taking a curl that falls gracefully beside her face, he twists it in his fingers.

"You make me feel beautiful, Edward."

He kisses her sweetly, but pulls back his desires to have the conversation they need to have before arriving home. "We need to talk, Celeste."

The passionate look is now replaced with a serious one. "What's wrong Edward?"

"Nothing my love, but we must talk about our plans, since we are almost home."

"Okay, what plans do we have?"

"I received a letter from your parents. With their decision to move to Virginia, they offered to sell us your family brownstone. What are your thoughts about that?"

Somewhat surprised, she didn't know how to respond. It would be wonderful living in a place she is already familiar with, but at the same time her parents won't be there. "Would you like that Edward?"

He says, "If you are okay with it, my love."

"I don't know that I would be comfortable with my parent's bedroom as ours," she says somewhat embarrassed that she thought about that.

He displays total understanding and compassion for her feelings. "We can take a look at redesigning the layout so that the master bedroom is located elsewhere. We'll stay at the Plaza until we complete the renovations. The current master suite can be the new guest suite. When your parents come to visit, they will stay in their own room. I will renovate to have our master suite on the main floor. Do you like that idea, darling?"

She replies, "Okay, I think that would work, but it will be strange living there with you instead of my parents."

"If you prefer not to, we can make other arrangements."

"No, let's do it. With the remodel, it should be very different, don't you think?"

"Yes, I will do everything to make it our own. I have also asked your father to search for a property for us near their new home. We can build a summer home there. Then you can visit anytime you wish."

"Thank you for that, Edward. I knew you would keep your word. Did my parents charge us a lot for the brownstone?"

"No, not at all," he replies smiling at her. "They were very fair with the price, quite low, in fact, for the value of it. They want you to be happy," he affectionately kisses the tip of her nose.

The whistle sounds, indicating they are pulling into port. As they approach the deck, she looks out at the city of New York. Celeste is glad to be home. She holds on to Edward's arm, while walking off the ship into her new life as Mrs. Edward Harrington.

The ride to the hotel is full of anticipation of the new life now before her. He holds her hand as they ride the streets of activity and excitement. Just being home reminds her of the changes that have now taken place in her life. She reflects. She is no longer a young virgin. She knows the facts of life, and what a man does to a woman in the privacy of their home. She is still self-conscious of what they do together in their bed. She really needs to speak with her mother to assure her that this is normal. The enjoyment and passion she and Edward share, explodes during their love making. Her heart is exploding with love for him as well. She is so happy.

She takes in the familiar things she has known all her life, but today she sees it differently. She watches the couples walk slowly down the street. Now, she examines them to see if she can tell if they have made love. She was always proper, never too close to Edward before, but now she wants to walk close to him. She wants to swim in his scent. She turns to look at him. He is gazing at her with adoring eyes. Who was she before Edward? She can't remember that naïve girl as she gazes into his eyes. As they pull up the drive to the hotel, she sighs deeply. Our new life begins now.

Stopping at the hotel door, employees greet him as he gets out. Together the staff and Edward unpack the car. Edward stops at the front desk to retrieve the keys to their suite. The desk clerk recognizes Edward and grabs them, handing the keys he announces, "Welcome, Mr. Harrington. I hope your trip was pleasant. Your suite is ready."

"Thank you," Edward says, taking the keys. "Please make sure we are not disturbed by housekeeping early each day. We will be staying here a few weeks and prefer the housekeeping to be completed while we are out."

The clerk replies, "Yes Sir, I will contact housekeeping immediately."

Edward thanks him then turns, taking Celeste's arm to guide her. They make their way to the Penthouse and quickly get unpacked. Edward takes a look at his pocket watch and decides it is time for dinner. "Would you like dinner in or out tonight?"

"We can dine in the hotel dining hall if that's okay with you?"

He replies, "Yes. We have been traveling so much. I don't quite feel like going out either."

They dine by candlelight in a dimly lit corner of the dining hall. He takes her hand in his and kisses it.

"Will it always be this way, Edward? I want to touch you every minute of every day. When I am away from you, I feel lost. How did I exist before you? How will I ever live without you again?"

"My darling, you will never have to find that out. Being apart is not an option for us. You are my wife forever and always."

As they stare into each other's eyes, Edward feels himself yearning to touch her. He quickly motions for the waiter, signing the bill. He takes her hand as they walk to the elevator. Inside the elevator, alone, he begins to kiss her, first softly then more heated.

"Edward, please stop." She laughs as she pushes him away. "Someone will see us."

"So? You're my wife. I can kiss you any time I please."

"Yes, Edward, but that is a kiss I know as a prelude to the something else."

He laughs out loud! "Yes my darling you are correct about that."

The elevator door opens, just as he reaches in for another kiss. She pushes him away seeing a couple waiting in the hallway. She blushes as they step off of the elevator. She scolds him for his public display of affection, all the while laughing into his sleeve.

Edward opens the door pulling her in swiftly. He backs her to the wall devouring her with kisses. Reaching for the top button on her blouse, he begins his seduction. The blouse is moderately low cut under her jacket. The matching ensemble is classy with a hint of suggestive appeal. He pushes the jacket off her shoulders and discards it onto the floor. He continues separating each button on the blouse as he kisses her mouth, then her neck, backing her toward the bed.

He has already removed his dinner jacket by the time they reach the bed. She unbuttons his shirt. Reaching a fevered pitch, they begin tearing clothes away like it's an emergency. The fire between them grows as their flesh meets in a raging flame of desire.

They fall to the bed like savages clawing each other. He knows she is ready. He enters her driving deep inside. She plunges into an abyss. She arches into him, riding the frantic rhythm of flesh meeting flesh. She climaxes and screams out-of-control with desire. She puts her arms around his back and rides with him over the edge. He moans loud as he releases, spent from exertion. Delirious, he falls down on top of her panting. He kisses her temple, then lays there with his face in the nape of her neck. "You are going to kill me," he groans out of breathe. She is quiet. He lifts his head and scrutinizes her.

"Edward, will it always be this way?"

"Darling, we are husband and wife. We can do anything together we please, for as long as we please. We are as one now."

"I know, I want this feeling to last forever."

"Good," he declares reaching over to kiss her. I want you to want to love me in every way. You are mine. I am yours. What would you like to do?"

She kisses him gently and he smiles.

He returns her kisses with warmth and longing. "I can't get enough of you, Celeste. I love you so much. God created you just for me."

"I agree," she snuggles into his arms.

They fall asleep depleted with exhaustion. Getting home from their trip, dinner, then love making spent them into a deep sleep.

CHAPTER 10

SETTLING IN

The next few weeks are busy with renovations at the brownstone. Her parents had moved out right after they left on their honeymoon. She went with Edward to buy furnishings for the home. Celeste's parents took all of their belongings with them to Virginia, or sold what they didn't want. They offered everything to Edward. Edward declined with thanks, telling them he wants Celeste to design her own home. He allows Celeste to select the new furnishings, directing her with suggestions to accommodate his business meeting needs. She has tastes that surprise and delight him. She furnishes the public areas with lavish décor, suited for their entertaining lifestyle. The private areas are decorated with romance and intimate settings in mind. Pictures of the two of them on their honeymoon are placed on the fireplace mantle in their bedroom. The bed is large to accommodate Edward's tall frame, yet cozy enough to provide the intimacy between them. The balcony doors are covered with sheers gathered at the top and bottom for privacy from the outside world, while still allowing enough light in to make the room open and airy. The kitchen area is the only place that doesn't require much attention. Her father had that perfectly designed for the staff. Sarah, her parent's kitchen aid, has family in New York, so they gave her the option to stay at the brownstone with Celeste and Edward, or move with the Morgan's to Virginia. Sarah chooses to stay at the brownstone. She is familiar with the kitchen, so she and Celeste make the decision to keep everything the same there. Soon, it's time to move in.

Her moving consists of the items she has at the hotel. Her belongings are still at the brownstone, from living there before.

Once the remodeling is complete, they move her things to the new location for the master suite. His move is a bit more extensive. His personal things are moved into the master suite. Edwards's business possessions are moved into the library, distinctly decorated for his working comfort. Both agree this will be perfect for the privacy he needs while working from home.

The wait staff helped a great deal in organizing and cleaning after the renovations. When Celeste and Edward arrive that afternoon, they walk into a beautifully decorated entryway. A small closet was built in the entryway to accommodate their winter outer wear. Entering, Edward helps Celeste off with her coat. She roams the area with great enthusiasm taking in the results. She enters the living quarters and sighs with pleasure.

"Edward. It is so beautiful! This is our home! I love it. It looks so different."

"I'm glad you're happy with it, my love. This is your home now, Celeste. You are the lady of the house, and I want you to feel that, not that it was your parent's home."

She walks through the room running her fingers on the small tables beside each sitting area. "I do. Nothing is like before. I can't wait for my parents to return, to see the changes."

Edward smiles, "I hope they will approve."

"I know they will." She turns around in circles joyfully taking in the whole room. "Edward when will we be able to visit my parents?"

Edward watches her and pauses with the answer, not wishing to disappoint her. "Let me get back up to speed with my business, to make sure it can function during my absence again. Once I do that we will make plans to visit them. Is that suitable? Can you wait a bit?"

"Yes, of course, Edward. Please take care of business first. I was thinking since it will be Christmas in a few months, we could plan a trip then. Would it be acceptable to send a letter giving them the date?"

He saw the excitement in her eyes, and could say nothing but, "Of course, my love."

She spends the next week sorting out the schedules for the staff, and becoming accustomed to Edward leaving for work each day. She thought she would be terribly lonely without her mother there. She finds being the matriarch of the house produces responsibilities that keep her busy throughout the day. She hadn't known her mother had so much to do. When she sits to write her family about the upcoming trip, she tells her mother about the tasks she has to do and compliments her on how easy she made it look all those years. "I never knew running a household could be so demanding," she tells her with enthusiasm. "I love it, mother. These wifely duties suit me. I was made to be Edward's wife." She continues the letter with questions about Virginia and how they are settling in.

After planning dinner, she goes in to freshen up for her husband. She bathes in lavender oils and dresses for dinner. She hears laughter coming from the living area and rings for the maid. "Do we have guests?"

The maid replies, "Yes, madame, I was just coming to tell you. Mr. Harrington has brought home a couple of business associates. He has asked for you."

"Well, I think we have enough food prepared with the arrangements we made for dinner, should he extend an invitation for them to join us. I wish he had warned me about their coming though." She returns to her closet selecting new attire to change into. Instead of the more romantic outfit she had planned, she will dress accordingly. "I'm sure this was unexpected," she tells the maid while selecting the more formal outfit.

She enters the room of guests wearing a long navy blue dress with a high lace neckline and matching lace at the wrist. The solid material falls midway between her knees, finishing off to the floor with blue and white ruffles and lace. It is gathered in the back with a coordinating ribbon. Solid blue material falls draping to the floor in gathers.

Edward turns to her as she enters the room. He beams with pride taking in her beauty. "Gentlemen, I would like you to meet Mrs. Harrington. Celeste, these gentlemen are business associates who stopped by the office this afternoon to offer their congratulations on our nuptials. I asked them over for drinks to meet you."

"Nonsense," she holds out her hand to greet them. "You must stay for dinner. We have more than enough prepared. Please, Edward, encourage them to stay."

Edward, appearing very surprised at his wife's pleasantries, insists the gentlemen stay. They accept doting on her graciousness.

During dinner, Edward watches as his wife reverently smiles at the conversations between the men. She has made his guests feel welcome showing appreciation of their stories. Again, he finds himself beaming over this beautiful woman.

Celeste laughs repeatedly when provoked by the stories told during the evening. She finds Edward staring at her at times. His eyes are filled with love. It is not missed by their guests who feel this couple is truly smitten.

After a glance of their affections, one of the gentlemen, Mr. Astor, lays his napkin on the table and pushes back his chair to stand. "Thank you for the wonderful evening, Edward, but I'm afraid it is time for us to take our leave. Thank you, Mrs. Harrington, for your gracious invitation to dinner."

"It was my pleasure, please come again, "she says as Edward pulls back her chair to rise.

The rest of the gentlemen provide their accolades as they take their leave one at a time, shaking Edward's hand. After their departure, Edward turns to playfully lift her up, twirling her around. "You are beautiful! You were wonderful tonight. I could not ask for a better partner than you my love. I expected you to be angry with me for bringing them home unannounced, but you were so gracious. I love you! You are my perfect equal. You complement me in front of my partners with your stunning nature and beauty."

Surprised at his glee, she doesn't quite understand his response to her actions. Her mother had always had these last minute gatherings, so she knew how to behave on such an occasion. She knew it was a wife's place to support her husband in all aspects of his relationships with business partners. Wives could make or break a deal by the reception in the spouse's home. Happy to see him so overjoyed, she joins in with the celebration of their successful night dancing and twirling. All rather quickly, their laughter and celebration turns to intimacy. Edward begins kissing her enthusiastically. She wraps her arms around his neck and pulls him in close. Celeste looks at him and raises her eyebrows with warning of things to come. He starts to move into her neck, but she turns away, taking his hand leading him to their room. She closes the door behind them rushing to kiss him deeply.

His head is spinning from the overindulgence of wine. The deep kiss plunges him immediately into full lustful surges. He hardens quickly. He removes his dinner jacket, vest and shirt. She is helping him undo his pants, wanting him, needing him. He unties the ribbon on the back of her dress. He removes the dress with quick intentions. Celeste is giggling with anticipation of their love making. It is an intense union. This time the respect that he gained tonight has made his love for her deeper. Edward desires her. The wine intensifies his feelings of lust. He pulls her to the bed feverishly kissing every part of her. Lying there in the darkness, their love reaches new heights. He is lying beside her breathing heavy from exertion from their lovemaking.

He reaches over to the bedside table, pouring some water into a glass. After he takes a drink, he hands it to her. Her mouth is dry, so she takes a drink then hands it back to him. He drinks the rest, setting the empty glass on the table. Turning onto his side to face her, he can see her through the moonlight. He reaches over and pulls her close. He kisses her sweetly, tenderly.

She returns his kisses and tells him she could never love anyone else or be with anyone else.

"Well, I should hope not," he laughs. "You're mine. No other man will ever touch you."

"No. I mean if you should leave me or die, I will never allow anyone to make love to me like you do."

He smiles, deciding this is good. "You will never be without me my love, that I can promise." He moves over to kiss her. Their lips and tongues seek each other causing overwhelming emotions to flood his heart. He thinks to himself how perfect she is. I can never get enough of her, and she gives everything I am willing to take.

CHAPTER 11

THE REUNION

It's only two weeks before the trip to see her parents. She's concerned that she will not be ready to leave due to the celebrations and entertaining with Edward's business associates. Tonight she is expecting thirty guests, the last social event before departing for her parents' home. She has prepared the menus and her staff is assisting her with the arrangements of each room. She has provided an area for an orchestra to play softly while still leaving enough room to dance. She stands back and takes in the beautiful room. She finally feels ready for the night.

Guests begin arriving at seven. Celeste and Edward greet them at the door while the staff takes their coats. The snow is falling, giving the night that extra holiday joy that accompanies a white Christmas. The fires are blazing in the fireplaces, with stockings hung from the mantles. Everyone enjoys the offered delicacies and drinks on the trays as they pass, replacing empty glasses with full ones.

Among the guests are socialites of New York who are dressed in elaborate tuxedos and gowns. As Celeste looks around, she is awestruck at the beautiful gowns the ladies are wearing. Many are low cut showing a fair amount of cleavage. Her gown, more revealing than normal, provides a respectful view of her assets. She is circled with ladies who provide lavish compliments of her home. "Thank you," she responds accepting the well-deserved praise. It was hard work to get everything perfect for this night. She appreciates the acknowledgement.

As guests roam in and out of lively conversations, she sees that Mr. Grayson joins their group. He is known around New York as a womanizer. Every woman in New York knows who he is, and many become melted pots of mush in his presence. He picks up in the conversation with light wit and humor. He is unusually handsome with a chiseled jaw, and dark eyes that penetrate the soul. The women are captivated with his good looks and hang on to his every word. He stares at Celeste, holds out his hand, and asks, "Would you honor me with a dance?" As she had danced with others, she did not hesitate to accept. They move gracefully around the floor to a slow waltz. His dancing skills are exceptional, putting her at ease right away; much different than some of the clumsy men she has had to endure throughout the night.

He whispers in her ear, "Celeste, you look lovely tonight, more beautiful than anyone in this room."

Used to compliments, she replies, "Thank you, Mr. Grayson."

"I am pleased that you accepted my dance invitation. May I expect another dance later in the night as well?"

She replies, "Of course, Mr. Grayson. The night is still young."

He flows into pleasant conversation that has her laughing as he tells of his many experiences at galas. Complimenting her on her dancing skills, he flatters her on her beauty and grace. As the conversation continues, he asks more personal questions about her father and his whereabouts. She tells him of their move to Virginia and their future trip to visit them.

"Ah, Virginia is a beautiful place. If I were to retire, that is where I would love to be as well," he gives an expression of great interest. "Virginia is almost as lovely as you. Your husband is a lucky man."

The conversation is consuming her. She doesn't realize the music has stopped, and a new dance has begun. She stops immediately upon realizing this, thanks him for the dance, then, leaves the floor. It would not be appropriate to dance more than one consecutive dance with anyone but her husband. She knows these strict standards, and could not believe she was that carried away with the conversation. He escorts her back to the group and quickly involves himself in the current discussions. The ladies are taking in his every word, falling at his feet. She watches him as he laughs, noticing the deep dimples, and his bedroom eyes. She looks around at the women who are smitten with him. She excuses herself from the group and makes her way to freshen up.

She decides to walk out on the balcony for some fresh air. She walks to the end of the balcony where no one is gathered. The snow is gently falling, providing a peaceful silence in the air. The music is seeping through the closed doors, providing a melancholy atmosphere. She feels a hand on her back. Quickly turning, she sees Edward smiling at her.

"Hello, my love. I have been looking everywhere for you," he kisses her lightly on her lips.

"Hi, darling. I needed a breather, so I stepped out for some fresh air. With the fireplaces and the large crowd, it's too warm. Are you enjoying the night?"

He replies, "Yes. It has turned out to be a very successful evening."

"Good," she says bringing her hand to his cheek. She suddenly shivers and pulls the shawl more tightly around her.

He says in a suggestive voice while pulling her into him, "Celeste, you are cold. Shall I warm you up?"

She laughs at his innuendo and moves into him for warmth. He lowers his head to hers taking her into a deep kiss. She responds then, quickly pulls away telling him he will mess up her makeup. "I can't go back into the party flushed from my husband's advances," she laughs as she purses her lips for a fake kiss.

"Better mine than another man's advances," he states.

She throws her arms around his neck and whispers, "There could be no other man in this world for me."

He pulls back and asks, "What about Mr. Grayson?"

She is rather shocked at the statement, "What? Why would you say something like that?"

"I saw how captivated you were with him on the floor. I must admit I felt a little jealousy creep in. Every woman here tonight is captivated by his good looks and charm."

She smiles at this. "Why Edward, I believe you really are jealous. Would I ever love anyone the way I love you? You have all of me, my love."

"Good response," he laughs at the absurdity of another man ever touching her.

They return to the brownstone when she catches, in the corner of her eye, Mr. Grayson leaning on the balcony rails. He is on the other side, almost out of sight. She glances at Edward to see if he has spotted him, but he doesn't show any signs of seeing him. For some reason, it felt uncomfortable to know he was there. What if Edward had not come out? Would he have made advances to approach her, having party-goers gossip about the contact? Had he been there the whole time watching? When Grayson was alerted that she had seen him, he nodded slightly. She did not respond.

Edward pulls her shawl off and lays it on a chair as they enter the room. He twirls her around merging into the dancers with ease. It is a slow graceful dance that allows him to whisper to her how much he loves her. She pulls back to view those blue eyes, then lays her head on his shoulder and closes her eyes. She dreams about later, when Edward will make love to her and the whole world will cease to exist. No one else matters, just the two of them.

He does not fail to wipe out the world that night, where he loves her with tenderness, then greedily takes her a second and third time.

The week of preparations for the trip ends quickly as they begin their journey to Virginia. The staff has packed their luggage and loaded everything into the vehicle taking them to the train. They leave on Monday by train in time for the gala on Friday celebrating the holidays. If they arrive by Wednesday, it will be time enough to rest and unite with her family. She is so excited. They plan to stay on the estate as she is told there is plenty of room for them.

Pulling into the estate, for the first time, she sees her parent's new home. It is beautiful and grand. She sees her mother and father waving with excitement. She jumps out of the car her parents had sent to pick them up, barely before it stops. Running to them, she throws herself into their arms. Tears well-up in her eyes. Her father grabs Edward's hand and pulls him into a man's back slap and says, "It is so good to see you, come on, let's get your luggage."

Celeste and her mother walk into the house, talking non-stop about how beautiful the house is. Elizabeth takes Celeste on the grand tour showing her the guest suite as she goes. "Your father and staff will assist Edward with the luggage and bring them here to your room."

"Did you do the decorating mother?"

"Your father and I made decisions on each area together. We discussed whether we wanted to change each room, or keep it the same, so the answer is, "Yes I did, but no I didn't in other spaces." She smiles about the dual answers. "How are you and Edward doing?"

"Mother, marriage is so wonderful. I love him more than I can tell you."

"Celeste, I'm so happy for you! I knew he was the one for you. He is a good man. So, you have settled into the brownstone?"

Celeste replies, "Mother, you would not recognize the place. We have changed almost everything. Your suite is now the guest room, so when you come to stay with us you will still be in your own room."

Celeste and her mother go off to talk for hours. She tells her mother all about the new person she has become as a mistress of the house. "The work is never ending," she says acknowledging the hard work her mother must have had to do before. "Mother, you made it look so easy. I never realized." Celeste catches her mother up on the happenings in New York, and her mother talks about the lifestyle in Virginia. "It is more relaxed than New York. No one is in a hurry," her mother explains. "This is a great place for retirement."

That night the table conversations were endless. One question after another went back and forth between the four.

Her father speaks to Edward, "I know you had mentioned a summer home here for you and Celeste so, before you return, I'd like to show you a property that would be perfect."

Edward smiles looking toward Celeste, and sees her excitement as he replies. "Sounds great, is it close by?"

"Yes, but it's on a mountainous road that ends in a one-eighty panoramic view of the valley. In fact, you can see our estate from there."

"Great, that sounds like an interesting investment."

Her father replies, "It would not be advisable to live there in the winter months. You could be snowed in. It's on a peak, not protected from the elements, so it would be very cold there during the winter months. I could see it becoming a nice summer home where the mountains are cooler."

"Sure. Let's take a look at it before we leave."

Friday comes all too fast. Celeste selects a dark-red dress commemorating the season of joy. She selects a ruby-red necklace to flatter the low-cut dress. The matching earrings dangle loosely to complement the ensemble. The corseted waist ends with gathers in the back cascading in layers. She glides gracefully down the stairs to meet Edward. He stands at the bottom with her coat, watching her as she descends. She takes in her very handsome husband in a black tuxedo, and falls in love with him all over again.

Edward thinks to himself, "She takes my breath away." He watches this beautiful woman walk toward him and still cannot believe how lucky he is that she loves him. Her strands of curls are pinned high on her head, but streams gradually down her back, with small ringlets framing her face. Her beautiful killer smile turns him into a lovesick puppy. "You are stunning," Edward takes her hand when she reaches the bottom step. He places her wrap over her shoulders, giving her a peck on the cheek. She takes his hand, walking to the parlor to meet her parents.

The party has already begun when they arrive. Edward recognizes many faces from New York. He is surprised that so many New Yorkers are attending. William knows many of the same businessmen, since they are both architects. He is surprised to see so many traveling so close to the holiday. Then again, why should he be surprised? Celeste's father was a very prominent man in New York. If you are invited as a guest on his list, you don't say no.

The four are served drinks as they enter the grand room where there is an Orchestra. A twenty-foot tall Christmas tree is the main focal point in the room. The Orchestra is playing softly, with the lights dimmed for ambiance. The four roam the crowd with Edward and William shaking hands and introducing Celeste and her mother, Elizabeth, to each group they encounter. The laughter and voices fill all corners of the room. Celeste feels excited. She is with her parents and the man she loves at the same time. She couldn't be happier.

William whispers into Elizabeth's ear. Taking her by the arm they proceed to walk on stage. Holding his wife's hand, he speaks to the crowd. "Thank you all for coming so far to share this wonderful holiday with us. My wife and family welcome you. Feel free to stop by our new home here in Virginia before you leave. Please eat, drink, and be merry. May God's blessings follow all of you throughout this holiday season, and throughout the New Year. Thank you!"

The crowd applauds, and gentlemen meet William at the bottom of the stage to shake hands and to share well wishes. Elizabeth and Celeste move from the crowd to find the table they are assigned. Seeing the seating labels, they place their drinks on the table. Celeste and her mother sit talking about everything. They discuss the dresses, the couples new and old, and the sadness of those who have passed this year. They are deep into conversations when a gentleman touches her shoulder and says, "May I have this dance?"

Celeste turns seeing Mr. Grayson holding out his hand to her. At first, she is stunned. She tries to recover from her startled surprise quickly. She hopes for her mother's support. Her mother instead, encourages her to dance. She didn't want to cause a scene so she stood and laid her hand in his.

"You seem surprised to see me, Mrs. Harrington. You did mention before that you would be here," he reminds her as they begin a slow back and forth dance.

She replies, "I have been surprised all night of the many New Yorkers who have made their way to Virginia during this holiday season."

"Your father is a very important man. When he sends an invitation, no one denies the request."

"I see. You must be an important man, Mr. Grayson," she says.

He searches her face looking for sincerity or sarcasm. His eyes move to her hair, then to her dress, making her uncomfortable. He remarks, "You are stunning as always, Celeste."

"Thank you, Mr. Grayson." She wants the dance to end. The music seems to go on and on, never ending. She is thinking about Edward's comments about him before, now wishing she hadn't accepted.

Mr. Grayson lifts her chin to look up at him, "Do I make you nervous, Celeste?"

She studies those dark eyes which seem to see right through her. She sees the dimples deepen as his grin widens. He is a very handsome man, and uses his charm to woo women. "Mr. Grayson, did you escort a young lady here tonight?"

"No, I'm alone." He smiles again deepening the dimples. "I prefer my time spent dancing with the most beautiful woman in New York and now Virginia."

She knew he was making an inappropriate pass at her. Just as she decides to end the dance, Edward taps Mr. Grayson's shoulder and asks, "Do you mind if I cut in? I would like to dance with my beautiful wife."

Mr. Grayson bows and backs away for Edward to step in. He makes his way through the crowd and leaves the floor rendering him out of sight.

Edward says nothing as the new dance begins. She says nothing as they continue to move slowly on the floor. She moves in closer to him gathering the scent of the man she loves. She melts into the comfort of his arms.

Edward finally speaks, "I would prefer you not dance with Mr. Grayson, Celeste."

Surprised, she looks up at him noticing his jaw is tightened. His eyes are avoiding hers, looking straight ahead.

"I wanted to say no, but mother insisted that I be polite and accept his request for a dance."

He replies, "I understand, but I am sensing he is interested in more than just a dance. I am a gentleman and cannot approach him with an accusation or show jealousy. What I do wish, however, is for you not to dance with him again. Have I made myself clear?"

"Edward! I am shocked at your tone with me right now. Do you think I have an interest in him?"

He studies her face, and just seeing those eyes, he melts. "I'm sorry, Celeste. I must be showing jealousy, and not expressing it appropriately, but when I see his hands on you, I can't take it. He is a lady's man, and is well known around New York for his scandalous ways."

"And you think I would be one of those women?"

He stops, looks down at her and says, "No, my love, of course not. I must sound like a fool. I have never felt this way. I just don't like him near you."

Trying to lighten his mood she pulls herself close to him and whispers in his ear, "I love you and only you, Edward. Shall I show you later just how much?"

He smiles deeply and says, "Oh yes, please show me how much you love me. You will need to show me more than once though. It will take some convincing. Will we be able to make love in your mother's house?"

"Yes, our room is all the way on the other side of the estate in a private wing," she says, happy that he is back to normal.

"Hhmmm" he moans, "How long before we leave?"

She laughs at his eagerness and says, "Not soon enough."

They leave the floor with Edward's possessive arm firmly around her small waist. They arrive back at the table, but find her mother and father nowhere in sight. Her father walks up saying, "Edward. I have someone I want you to meet."

He looks at Celeste, and she motions for him to go on. She will be okay, so he leaves with her father.

Chad Grayson is standing in full view of Edward and Celeste. He doesn't know why he is so taken with Celeste. When Edward leaves her at the table, he is tempted to walk back over to her but decides not to push his luck. Edward displayed possessiveness when he asked to cut in. He doesn't want to offend a business associate, but nonetheless, he cannot get her off his mind. Her scent is captivating. He has never had a woman not succumb to his chivalry and charm. It is clear she is dedicated to Edward. She's a challenge that makes him want her more. He grabs another young lady. Taking a turn on the floor, he decides to let it rest for now.

Celeste is busy conversing with other ladies when Adrianna walks up to the group. Adrianna has been her best friend since they were children. She is stunning with velvet black hair and dark thick lashes. She is dressed in a dark-green gown that hugs her perfect figure. Celeste squeals with excitement when she sees her! They hug and run off together to talk.

Finding a small corner away from the noise, Celeste squeals, "I have so much to tell you Adrianna! Married life is wonderful. You must try it!" she laughs out loud.

Adrianna giggles, "Tell me. Tell me. What is married life like?"

Celeste goes into the tirade of information, how it was difficult to sleep with him at first. Having a man in bed near her was something she had to get used to. He wants to make love every night," she gushes then blushes. "It's all so wonderful. I want you to come by when we get back to New York. We have completely changed the brownstone. You won't recognize it. When did you get back from Paris?"

Adrianna tells her about her trip to Paris for the last six months. "My mother and I left right after your wedding."

"I was wondering why you hadn't come by."

Just as Celeste was about to ask the next question, they are interrupted by Mr. Grayson.

He holds out his hand, "Celeste, may I have this dance?"

Feeling somewhat frustrated at his persistent advances, she replies, "Hello, Mr. Grayson. I would like you to meet my best friend, Adrianna Vanders. We are catching up after some time apart."

Mr. Grayson turns toward Adrianna and takes her hand, "It is a pleasure to meet you, Ms. Vanders." She is just as stunning as Celeste, he thinks to himself. He wonders why he hasn't seen this one around New York. "Ms. Vanders, are you a native of New York? I don't believe I have had the pleasure of your acquaintance before."

Adrianna replies, "Yes. I was born and raised in New York."

Suddenly, it comes to him. Wow, has she changed from his memory of her. The Vanders are moguls around New York.

Trying not to be too obvious, he questions her. "Does your father own the extravagant home on the outskirts of Manhattan?"

"Why, yes, the Vanders Estates," she says seeing his expression that he knows the place.

Getting back to his purpose, he turns to Celeste asking for the dance again.

Knowing there is no way she would dance with him after Edward's tirade; she makes an excuse and encourages Adrianna to join him.

He politely turns to Adrianna and holds out his hand, "It would be my honor if you would join me."

Adrianna smiles and puts her hand out to his.

They stroll to the floor hand-in-hand. The music begins with a fast waltz. Celeste watches the two in amazement that they moved as if they had danced together before. They are a striking couple. She makes her way back to her table where her mother is returning from a dance with an old partner of William's.

Elizabeth thanks him for the dance and turns to Celeste as she approaches. "I don't think I can dance one more dance. My feet are killing me."

Only minutes pass when Edward approaches the table. "Are you ready to leave, Celeste? Your father says he will be here for a while yet, and says to take his car." He tells Elizabeth, "William said to offer you a ride home with us if you are tired."

"Oh, yes. I am very tired and would love to leave with you and Celeste."

"I will get your wraps, and meet you at the door," Edward kisses Celeste lightly as he leaves.

Elizabeth comments, "The two of you look so happy, Celeste. Are you?"

"Yes mother. I am so very happy."

On the drive back to the Morgan's, they discuss everything and everyone. Edward drives in silence listening to his wife chatter on with her mother as if they were best friends. He decides that he must find a summer house for her here. She needs to spend these happy times with her mother. He hates they are apart because of him.

He parks and escorts both ladies into the house. Elizabeth excuses herself and says she must get out of her shoes and clothes. "I will see both of you in the morning." She hugs her daughter and leaves.

"Good night. I love you."

Edward and Celeste make their way to their room. She moans, "I'm exhausted."

Edward closes the door and grins, "Not too exhausted I hope. You assured me this is the privacy wing."

"Yes, my love, very private," she whispers.

He replies, "If walls could talk."

CHAPTER 12

RETURN TO LOVE

Edward and Celeste stay with her parents until after the New Year. On New Year's Eve, the Morgan's home is filled with visitors. Many invited guests for the gala don't return to New York right away. The local hotels are booked due to their event. Elizabeth and Celeste meet the wives for lunches, and even host events for the ladies at the estate. The many couples gather for daily planned activities. The men are always discussing business while the women enjoy socializing.

The day after the holidays, Edward goes with William to see the property he mentioned earlier in the week. Edward is fascinated with the view from the mountain and loves it. He takes Celeste up to see the property later that day, and they both agree it's perfect. He contacts his attorney to make an offer on the property. It is accepted after just one day. A spring date is set for construction to begin. It will make a great winter project for Celeste and Edward, to design the summer home. Selecting everything to build this house will be an exciting adventure, an undertaking that will take two years to complete. Edward decides on marble stone. Items will need to be shipped in from other areas out of the country causing great delays.

The next few years are full of joy. Celeste's and Edward's love has grown immensely. They have moved into a romantic love. There are nights of fine wine and intimate dinners that end in tender lovemaking. Their love can still be raging, but there is sweetness now about their touch. His touch is not always fiery, but gentle and soft. He gazes at her with eyes that reveal his affectionate emotions. She sees him as her life. She waits impatiently for him to return from work each day, longing to be close, to hear his laughter. The humor between them is full of banter and feistiness. They finish each other's sentences. They are so in sync. Neither have doubts and insecurities that some couples go through. It was their destiny to be together. As time passes, their love travels to depths of emotions unparalleled by any they know. Their love builds a bridge over time that even death cannot separate.

Spring, two years later, they are finally completing the construction. The hustle and bustle of placing orders and hiring contractors to build the summer home has been endless. They had to make quite a few trips to the property during that time to meet with contractors, giving great opportunity for Celeste to visit her family. Edward keeps adding requirements, making the building of the house extremely detailed. He also decides at the last minute to build a power house right on the property to accommodate their electrical needs. He wants electric lights available in all rooms. Electric bulbs will take a lot of electricity to burn, so he wants to be prepared for that. Fireplaces are built in every room for heating purposes.

As the manor takes shape, it's finally ready for their move in by mid-summer. Finalizing it is taking a lot of Edward's time. They are invited by some friends to attend a large picnic. Needing to make up time at work for time away in Virginia, Edward encourages Celeste to go without him. She decides to attend. She rings for the driver and car and travels the short distance to the Vander's home, near downtown Manhattan, on the outskirts of town. The Vander's home is gorgeous. As Celeste pulls onto the property, she gets excited about her own Virginia property. She can't wait to have a house like this one, in Virginia. She arrives and gets out of the car and makes her way to the back yard estate. When she arrives, she sees rows and rows of tables set up with food. She had never seen a more exquisitely catered affair.

She walks around meeting guests while enjoying the beautiful weather. She sees a stream down below the hillside and decides to take a stroll. Walking a distance away, she notices beautiful benches under the shade of a tree. She stops to sit and enjoy the evening. In her peacefulness, she watches the waters flow by.

"How are you, Celeste?" The deep voice startles her. She turns to see Chad Grayson hovering over her.

She stands quickly, "I am well, thank you. I should be getting back to the festivities." As she begins to pass him, he grabs her arm.

"Please, Celeste. May I speak with you for just a moment?"

She replies, "I don't think we have anything to discuss. We are all alone Chad." She motions toward the guests on the hill.

"I understand, but I will only take a minute of your time."

She hesitates, but obliges his request. She walks back over to the bench and sits down. "What is it, Mr. Grayson?"

He observes her as his heart pounds fast, trying to get the words out. "I am not a bad person, Celeste, but I find I have been captivated by you. I measure every woman I meet against you. Your beauty and grace are always in my thoughts. Recently, I have tried my best to avoid you on every occasion as not to make a fool of myself."

"Mr. Grayson, I am a married woman. Please, this is not appropriate."

"I understand that, Celeste, but please hear me out."

"Okay, you have only a moment to finish."

"Let me begin by saying I have had no plans to interfere with your marriage. I know you love your husband. That is what has made you more appealing, if that is even possible. Edward walks around with such pride having you on his arm. I can tell he knows how lucky he is. I just need to tell you the feelings I had for you were real. I am not trying to make a pass at you, but to just honestly tell you how I have felt."

"Mr. Grayson."

"Please call me Chad."

"Mr. Grayson, thank you for your flattery, but I really don't understand why this needs to be said when you know I am happily married."

He hesitates, thinking a moment. "I don't know why either, Celeste. I just need to say it. I have thought many times that I was in love with you."

Just as Celeste was about to reply, Adrianna walks out from behind the tree and screams, "How dare you! How could you be involved with the man I love?" Adrianna looks at Chad with sadness and anger. Removing her ring from her finger, she throws it at him. She turns to leave, but Chad catches her.

Holding her by the arm Chad yells, "Just listen to me!"

She jerks her arm away from him and says, "I have heard enough to know you are telling a woman other than me that you love her!"

"Wait just a minute Adrianna!" He continues, "You can't just walk up on one little piece of a conversation and think you know the rest!"

Celeste is now in a panicked state. "Please Adrianna, you are misunderstanding the conversation. Please don't go. I do not return any of his feelings. You have to know that!"

Chad looks at Celeste and tells her sadly, "That is true Adrianna. She has never had feelings for me other than friendship."

Adrianna scrutinizes him with tears welling in her eyes. "Then it is you who is in love with her." She states it and brings her hand to her mouth in horror.

He grabs Adrianna by the hand and pulls her to the bench across from Celeste. "No, that is not what I am trying to say. If you had heard the conversation prior to the last part you would have heard a lot of past tense statements. At one time, I truly thought I was in love with Celeste. Until the night I met you, I felt obsessed with her. I couldn't get her out of my mind. I measured every woman I met to her, and no one came close. Then I met you Adrianna. I was trying to get to that point when you walked up. My life changed the moment Celeste introduced us. It changed my life. You made me whole for the first time."

Adrianna sat staring at him as if she didn't believe what he was saying. "That is not what I was hearing when I walked up."

Chad grabs her hand in his, "That's the point I was trying to make to her. Up until that night, Celeste had my heart. So much so I thought I was in love with her. I was trying to explain my feelings for you, Adrianna. The night I met you changed the feelings I had for Celeste. You are wearing my ring. I gave you my heart! I was trying to thank Celeste in the best way I knew how. Without her, I would never know the kind of love I could feel. I wanted what Edward had. I was sure the only way I could ever find that love was with Celeste. I have been a womanizer since I can remember. Celeste was always this one woman I could never have. I did think at one time I was in love with her." He hesitates, looks at Celeste, then back at Adrianna. "Then, I met you. Without those feelings I had for Celeste, I would never have known the kind of love Celeste and Edward have, not until now."

Celeste completely understands what Chad has been trying to tell her. She had not allowed him to finish his words. "Adrianna, Chad has always been a perfect gentleman to me. He knows I am married, and has never interfered with that. I do believe he loves you, Adrianna."

Chad takes Adrianna's hand and puts the ring back on her finger. Adrianna's eyes well up with tears. "I love you, Chad. Are you sure you are over Celeste?"

He smiles, and his dimples deepen. Adrianna melts as she always does. "I love you." He takes her in his arms and kisses her deeply.

Celeste seizes the moment and climbs the hill back to the guests. Whew, she thought, what a day! Suddenly, feeling sick, she decides to leave. Thinking it is the biscuit she ate for breakfast, or the drama of the day, she departs without notice.

CHAPTER 13

A TINY GIFT

By the time Celeste reaches her house, she is wrenched with nausea. She drinks some warm tea then lies down. Edward comes home at seven that evening to find her in bed. Concerned, he gets her a small piece of bread and some water to help settle her stomach. He sits with her on the bed until he sees she is feeling better. "It may help if you get some food in your stomach. What have you had to eat today?"

Thinking about the day, she realizes, due to the commotion with Mr. Grayson and Adrianna, she has not eaten anything except for a small biscuit early that morning. She decides, "Now that I think about it, you may be right. Let me wash my face. I'll meet you downstairs in a moment."

He kisses her on the forehead and leaves the room.

Celeste washes her face, and combs her tangled hair. Gazing in the mirror she sees she is pale. Pinching her cheeks, she goes down stairs to meet Edward.

"Hi darling, you look much better. Are you feeling okay?"

"I do feel a little better," she checks her stomach for nausea. "I think you are right. I haven't eaten much today, so that may be what's wrong."

Dinner is served and, as expected, she begins to feel better. After a bite or two, she says, "This is exactly what I needed."

Edward tells her during dinner everything that has been accomplished this week at the Virginia home. "We need to begin shopping for the furnishings now. Should we buy things here or shop in Virginia?"

She replies, "I think we should visit some Virginia homes to see what the style is for the area and where they purchased their furnishings. Mother and Father designed their new home much different than their home here in New York."

"You're right. Do you want to plan to leave for Virginia next week? We can stay at your parents."

"Yes, Edward. That sounds perfect." As the conversation lulls, she knows she needs to discuss with Edward what occurred at the Vander's today. At the same time, she wants to avoid the topic.

"Darling, you haven't said a word about your outing today at the Vanders. How did that go?"

Beginning slowly, now realizing the topic is at hand, she tells him, "Honestly, I didn't stay that long with my illness. I began feeling sick soon after I arrived." She hesitates, "But there is something that happened that I need to discuss with you."

Edward hears the tone in her voice change, so his curiosity is piqued by her statement. "What's with the serious tone?" What is it, Celeste?"

Celeste begins the story. "I ran into Mr. Grayson today."

Immediately Edward gets tense and strongly says, "What did he do?"

She relays the event to him. Before she could get to the main point, Edward, just like Adrianna, was fuming. "I am going to deal with this once and for all. I have been tolerant, but I will not have another man tell my wife he loves her." He moves to get up from the table but she grabs his arm.

"Please, Edward, let me finish!"

Angrily, he sits back down and waits for her to continue. When she has relayed the whole story, Edward is surprised with the outcome. "Adrianna is engaged to him?"

"Yes, they have been together for the past six months. We have been missing them around town. I guess we haven't been to many functions lately with our travels to Virginia."

"But we should have heard some kind of an announcement around town."

"I know. You would have thought so, but I think it just happened," she shrugs her shoulders. "I am so happy for them."

Edward raises his eyebrows to her, "I'm not so sure he is right for her. Admitting his feelings for you makes him a scoundrel in my book."

"Edward, you have missed the whole point. He wanted a love like ours! It is such a compliment to you and to me. He thinks of us as the perfect couple and wanted that for his own life."

"I just don't trust the man. I have not liked him since he focused all of his attention on my wife, and you shouldn't either, Celeste. Adrianna is your best friend. He could hurt her deeply."

"Edward, I believe him. He was so forthcoming today. I saw the love in his eyes for Adrianna. She is deeply in love with him, too."

Edward lays his hand over hers, "I hope you are right, Celeste, for Adrianna's sake."

She leans over to kiss him. "I love you, my wonderful, perfect husband."

He returns her kiss, then another one, then another one. "Hhmmm, "This wonderful, perfect husband wants to make love to his wife. Does wonderful and perfect wife feel the same way?"

She smiles, "Yes, let us make perfect love!" They fill their tub for bathing. Sipping wine, they lie in each other's arms until very late in the night. Sleep is delayed by perfect love making.

The next morning, Celeste wakes up retching. Edward becomes concerned. "Darling, I'm calling the doctor."

"Edward, I think we just over indulged in the wine last night."

He pulls her hair back from her face. She is drenched with sweat. "Honey, you have a fever. I'm calling the doctor."

The doctor arrives by ten o'clock. He dismisses Edward from the room to examine her. He comes out of her room a half-hour later, stops in front of the hall table to don his jacket, and to buckle his medicine bag.

Edward hears him and hurries to the hallway. "How is she? What's wrong with her, doctor? Is it serious?"

"Slow down, take a deep breath, Edward." He gives him a big wide grin. "I think your wife has something to tell you."

Confused, Edward starts toward the door. Before he passes him, the doctor shakes his hand. "Go on in, she will be alright."

Edward rushes through the door of her room. "What's wrong, Celeste? The doctor said you are okay, but didn't say what was wrong. Is it the flu?"

Smiling from ear to ear, she says, "Yes, darling, a flu that will last nine months." She watches his face as it changes from confusion to full understanding.

"Oh my God! We're having a baby," he yells in an emotional outburst.

Celeste looks at him showing no emotions at first, then screams, "We're having a baby!"

He falls on the bed grabbing her. He kisses her all over her face, then her mouth, back to her face again. "Darling, this is wonderful news."

She agrees, "It's the best time to find out. We are visiting my parents next week. It will be wonderful news to give them."

Edward lays his hand on her stomach, "Darling, will you feel up to a trip to Virginia?"

"The doctor tells me its morning sickness. By afternoon, I should be okay. We'll just take it slow until the morning nausea has subsided."

"Okay, that will work. We'll go over to my parent's right before we leave to break the news to them. They will be ecstatic. My mother has been non-stop asking when she will be a grandmother."

"That's a great plan," she says kissing him softly.

Edward gazes into her eyes, "My darling. I love you more than life itself. Thank you so much for giving me a child. Our love will be growing inside you." He lays his hand on her stomach and kisses her.

"Our perfect life will now include a perfect baby!"

CHAPTER 14

BABY MAKES THREE

Before Celeste and Edward leave New York, they go by his parent's house to deliver the good news. His parents are beside themselves with joy. They begin immediately pampering Celeste. "Celeste, get off your feet. Sit here, it's more comfortable."

Celeste looks at Edward and smiles warmly, appreciating his parent's joy. She humorously says, "I need to get pregnant more often. I could get used to this attention." His mother starts telling Celeste all about her pregnancy with Edward. Everyone is in high spirits. Celeste and Edward break the news regarding their trip to Virginia.

Edward's mother questions them, "Should you really be traveling with Celeste in this condition?"

"Yes, we need to see her parents in person to deliver the news. The doctor says she has morning sickness. We will be on the train so she will rest when she needs to." After a few debates about the safety, they embrace and leave arriving in Virginia a few days later.

Celeste's parents are overcome with joy. Her mother screams with excitement at the news. As with his parents, Celeste's comfort was foremost on her parents' minds.

The next day, after lunch, Edward, Celeste, along with her parents, visit the Virginia home construction site. Edward had asked her father to watch over the construction of the build while they were in New York, so William has a lot to show them.

Entering the house, the very wide staircase looms large and regal. To her surprise, at the top of the stairs is a stained-glass window of her! She looks at Edward and says, "Who did this?"

"I hired someone to do it. Do you like it?"

She walks slowly up the stairs, taking in each detail. "Edward, it makes me look beautiful. I'm nowhere close to that image."

Edward disagrees, "I beg to differ, my love. It is in the same image of the portrait over our mantle."

She now sees the details of that portrait. "You're right."

"I had the artist of the original portrait work alongside the glass company to sketch it. I wanted it to be identical to the portrait at home," he declares with pride.

She looks up at Edward, sees the love in his eyes, and says, "I'm so blessed to be your wife."

Celeste's father takes them from room to room relaying the details of construction for Edward and Celeste.

They go through rooms making notes for ordering its contents. A nursery was added close to the master suite with a neutral decorated theme to update later for the sex of the child; boy or girl. The servants' quarters will not be in the main living area. Edward wants the live-in servants to also have their own families with them so he built a whole section of the manor just for them. They will, of course, be close at hand, but not twenty-four hours a day. She wants their lives to be as normal as possible. They will clean, serve meals, and assist with events held in the main house. Celeste will have a nanny for the baby once it's here. The nanny's room will be at the end of the hall. Although the servants live with them, she wishes them to treat their responsibilities as a job. At the end of each day, go home, just as Edward does each day.

Standing in front of the finished home, she is amazed at its beauty. Edward watches smiling, "Are you happy with the finished product?"

"Edward, it's beautiful. We have to name it."

"I already have." Edward announces the name with pride, "Celestial Manor."

She looks at him with disbelief. Tears well up and begin to fall.

Edward, seeing her emotion asks, "What's wrong honey?"

"I don't know if it is hormones with the pregnancy, but I feel so emotional. I love the name. You are the best husband in the world. I always know your love because you show it every day."

She reaches up to him and holds his face between her hands. She lightly kisses his lips.

He brushes away her tears, and pulls her into him. They stand embraced in silence, taking in their beautiful new home.

Her parents watch their daughter and her husband. They are delighted with the man she has married. A father could wish no better for their daughter than the man here before them.

After the grand tour, the four collaborate to find the perfect look for its furnishings. She knows mahogany is the wood theme that they both agree on. They visit locals that Celeste's father has made friends with to check out their décor. The ladies are happy to take Celeste through their homes.

After a week, everything is either purchased or ordered to be made. They spend a few more days visiting her parents, then head home.

The morning sickness subsides after two months, but exhaustion is the new normal. Although tired a lot, things have gotten back to normal. The August heat doesn't help with the drained feelings. They are not able to travel to Virginia with her condition. They take the time to settle in, and enjoy the pregnancy. Her father and mother are meeting the deliveries at Celestial Manor. All is well.

One night in mid-September, they have readied themselves for bed. When she emerges from her bath Edward watches her, "Is it possible for you to be more beautiful each and every day?" He rubs his hand over the big mound of her belly as she sits beside him on the bed.

"I must admit I feel a certain glow, Edward. I walk into the nursery every day. I can't wait for our baby to arrive."

He comforts her, "November will be here before you know it."

"Not for me" she says, rubbing her belly softly. "It seems like forever."

"I promise, love, it will be short. What we need to do is enjoy our time together now while we are alone. Once our bundle gets here, life will be very demanding for you. You don't want to neglect your very needy husband do you?" He rubs her belly, but quickly moves to her breasts. "Hhmmm, these have grown quite a bit."

She laughs, "Oh and how I know it. They are huge. My back is killing me," she moans looking down at them. "But I know you love the size!"

He stares at the mounds of breasts that are now making his mind go where it always does when she is near. Even at seven, almost eight months of pregnancy, his lust for her has not diminished. He has only to see Celeste and his heart races. His love has not only grown physically for her, but his emotions are tied up in her. At times, he finds he can't focus at work, wanting to get home to her. She is carrying his child. The ultimate gift of their love is growing inside her. He kisses her and she responds willingly, letting him know she is feeling well enough to engage.

She whispers, "I feel so heated when you touch me, hotter than ever before."

That is all it takes for Edward to take the moment and turn it into a passionate exchange. Ravishing her, they both go over into splendor and satisfaction. They fall completely spent and exhausted. As she lay in his loving arms, she could never have imagined how wonderful it would be with her husband. He satisfies her in every way, both in and out of bed.

The next two months are spent with tender nights of lovemaking. Her frequent lustful desires have made her more aggressive in what she wants from him.

It is a cold winter's night in November. They are sitting together in the parlor on the sofa. Waiting for her parents to arrive from Virginia for Thanksgiving, she feels her large round belly tighten. At first, she thinks the baby is moving, but when it happens a second time, she lays her hand at the bottom of her stomach to feel it tighten again. She grabs Edward's hand and says, "Feel this honey. I have never felt this before."

He lays his hand where she places it, but feels nothing. "I don't feel anything."

"It stopped," she shrugs it off thinking it was just the baby moving.

Twenty minutes later, it happens again. "Honey, it's happening now."

He reaches over to lay his hand on the area, but once more, feels nothing.

Twenty minutes, it happens again. "Honey, I think I may be going into labor."

He sits up straight, "Does it feel like contractions?"

"Yes." They decide to start timing them. She ponders more thoughtfully, "It may be contractions, since I have never had a baby, I don't know what it feels like."

"Let's see what timing tells us. The doctor says to watch for consistent or increases in discomfort. That will most likely be labor."

They time the contraction for three more hours, until they are ten minutes apart. He decides, "I think we need to get to the hospital honey. Let's at least get you checked to see if this is normal."

Celeste is feeling frightened. After all the wishing, the time is at hand and she finds herself not ready.

Suit case already packed, they call for the car to take them to the hospital. Edward calls his parents to let them know what is going on. Her parents are on their way to New York, so they couldn't reach them. He leaves a message with the staff to let her parents know to come to the hospital when they arrive. They are hopeful everyone arrives in time for the birth.

After Dr. Mason examines her, he says, "Celeste, you are definitely in labor. Your contractions are two minutes apart. We are going to get you down to the delivery room to prepare you for birth. Edward, there is a private waiting room for the family." He motions for the attendant to escort them to it. As they are leaving the room, Celeste's parents arrive. Her mother rushes in to give her a kiss before they take her down to the labor room.

"Thanks, Doc." Edwards says running his fingers through his hair with worry. "Is she okay? I mean is everything going as it should?"

"Yes, Edward. She is at seven centimeters dilated, and her water has broken. It broke during the exam. Since her water has broken, things should move along quickly now."

Edward asks, "What is full dilation?"

Dr. Mason answers, "Ten. Everything is right on track."

Edward and their parents follow the attendee to the private waiting room. In less than an hour, Dr. Mason returns. Removing his surgery cap, he says, "It's a girl!"

Edward jumps up and yells! He grabs his parents and her parents, and hugs them with enthusiasm. "When can I see her?"

"They are cleaning them up now. You can see them in about thirty minutes," the doctor says with a big grin on his face. "Congratulations, Dad!"

Edward turns back to the parents and yells, "I'm a dad! On November 21st, 1914, I'm a father!"

Edward goes in first, alone with Celeste and their newborn daughter. Celeste is in the bed with daughter in her arms in a pink blanket. He kisses Celeste lightly on the cheek, then, leans down to kiss the baby on top of her head. "She is beautiful," he says as he sits in front of them.

"She is, isn't she?" Celeste gazes into the adoring face of their child. "Are we still going with the name we picked out? Does she look like a Catherine to you?"

"Yes, darling, Catherine is a beautiful name." He kisses Catherine, then Celeste. "I'll go get our parents. They are anxiously waiting to see both of you. The doctor is allowing them in just for a minute." He leaves and returns with them. His mother and father, and her mother and father push into the room beaming. The mothers are gushing over the adorable baby girl.

Celeste's mother asks, "Are you okay, honey?"

"Yes, mother. I feel fine. The delivery was very fast."

Her father comes over and kisses her on the forehead. "Congratulations, darling."

"Thank you, father. Isn't she adorable?"

He looks lovingly at the infant in his daughter's arms, "Both of you are adorable." He turns and pats Edward on the back.

His parents are standing on the other side of the bed. Catherine's tiny fingers are wrapped around Edward's mother's finger. Celeste looks up at her, then both reach and embrace. His mother says to her, "Thank you so much for my beautiful grandchild."

Celeste, through a stifled cry, says, "Thank you for allowing me to marry your son." Their embrace tightens. They are a family that loves without end.

CHAPTER 15

TIL DEATH DO US PART

Eight years later in the spring of 1922, Celeste and Edward arrive at Celestial Manor for the summer. They spend fall and winters in New York, but the spring and summer months are enjoyed in the cool hills of Virginia. They pull up exhausted by the trip. Her parents are sitting outside with a cold glass of tea when they arrive. Both rush to meet them as Celeste and Edward get out of the car.

"Hi mother," Celeste says getting out of the car as her parents walk toward her. William opens the back door of the car to get to the sleeping Catherine, sprawled out on the back seat. Catherine is eight years-old now, quite the little lady. She has her mother's beauty, but the dark features of her father.

"Hello, darling," her mother gives her a big hug. "You look tired. Was it an exhausting trip?"

Edward circling the car informs them that they made good time. "Traffic wasn't too bad. With the warm weather, we really enjoyed the ride with the windows open and the cool breeze." He hugs his mother-in-law and pats his father-in-law on the back glancing down at Catherine still sound asleep in his father-in-law's arms. "Nothing wakes her," he laughs as he pulls the luggage from the trunk. They all walk up the step to the entryway.

Entering into the main living area, William lays Catherine on the couch, placing a throw over her to warm her from the chill of the air. He walks over to give Celeste a kiss on the cheek. After giving him a warm affectionate hug, she walks to an oversized chair and sinks into it lazily. "It was a beautiful ride, but a very exhausting couple of days," she sighs.

Elizabeth enters the room with tea and a tray of cheese and crackers and sits it on the center table. "Here, honey. This should hold you over until dinner is ready. After this, you should go up and take a hot bath. A bath will refresh you."

Edward walks over and takes a glass from the tray, handing one to Celeste as well. Examining Celeste, seeing her exhaustion, he tells her, "That bath sounds like a good idea, honey. I might do the same."

Both Edward and Celeste retire to their bed chamber to bathe and change into comfortable clothes. When they return downstairs, they find Catherine sitting on William's lap. Elizabeth is lighting candles on the long dining table. Dinner has been prepared by the staff and is ready for their meal.

The men catch up on business during the meal while the women talk about what is going on in the area. Celeste instructs the nanny to put Catherine to bed. It's after nine when Elizabeth and William leave for home. Celeste and Edward relax.

Celeste is seated on the couch when Edward brings a glass of red wine to her. "Here darling, this should relax you for bedtime."

She takes the glass thanking him and takes a sip. She lays her head back on the couch and closes her eyes. "It has been a long day."

Edward sits beside her and agrees, "It has been." He observes the room, admiring the beauty of it and says, "It's always worth it though. I love this place. It's so far away from the stress of work. I always need the relaxing time we spend here."

She searches his handsome face. It is the most handsome face she has ever seen. Seeing the fatigue in his eyes, Celeste nuzzles close to him, planting a kiss. "Let's get some rest. We'll feel better tomorrow." She stands, pulling him up with her. They walk arm and arm up the wide staircase to their suite. They go directly to bed and quietly fall asleep in each other's arms in minutes.

The next morning, feeling refreshed, they go downstairs together around nine o'clock. The sun is bright, shining through the very large windows. The sashes are up, and the breeze is blowing the curtains. The fresh air is crisp, filling the room with a floral scent. Edward takes in a deep breath and sighs, "Ah, fresh air."

Catherine comes bounding down the steps with a doll baby in her arms followed by the nanny. "Look, mommy and daddy, I woke up with this in my arms. Isn't my baby pretty?"

They had forgotten her doll in New York. Edward suggested stopping by a store to purchase her a new one. It was Edward's brilliant idea. Celeste shoots him an approving smile. "You were right." Celeste didn't think that would pacify her, but this shows she was wrong.

Edward gets very excited about the new doll, while Catherine gleefully kisses the doll repeatedly. "What's her name?" Edward asks.

Catherine examines the doll, and a puzzled look appears on the innocent face. "I don't know, daddy."

"Well, I think we should name her now," He is still showing interest in the baby-sized doll.

"What about Baby?" she asks, taking in the infancy of the doll.

Edward quizzes her, "You don't want to give it a real name?"

"No, I like Baby. She looks like a baby."

"Well, Baby it is!" He thoughtfully looks down at the doll, "Hi, Baby! Welcome to the family."

Celeste insists, "Okay, you two. Please come to the table for breakfast. It's getting cold.

They enjoy breakfast then take a long walk on the property. "It's so beautiful here," Celeste declares looking up at her husband who is admiring the scenery.

"It is, my love. There is so much peace."

Catherine is running back and forth in front of them, falling and rolling on the ground. They laugh, admiring the energy she displays.

Edward gapes at Catherine and goes deep into thought. After a time of silence, he says, "Celeste, I want to have another baby."

She stops, surprised at this new interest in another child. "What brought this on?"

"I have been thinking about it a lot lately. I was planning to discuss it with you this summer. I guess now is as good a time as any. I know we have been undecided for a long time, but before we get too old, let's have another one."

Thinking about it for a moment she replies, "I want another one if you do."

"Good, then let's practice making babies," he whispers romantic suggestions in her ear.

She hits him on the arm and tells him he is shameful.

He lays his head back and releases a deep roaring laugh. After he stops laughing he teases, "You know you want me."

She again hits his arm and laughs sheepishly. Looking at him with so much adoration, she feels her heart swell with love. "What would I ever do without your mischief?"

He replies, "You will never find out. I will be mischievous until the day I die."

Those words echo in her mind. "Die." Her mind goes to a place her heart could not travel. If anything were to ever happen to Edward, she would not want to live.

Edward sees the seriousness on her face. He says, "I am too mischievous to die! You will have to deal with me forever." He kisses her deeply.

Catherine bounces up between them and grabs their hands. "I'm hungry."

Pulling his pocket watch, he announces, "Wow, we have been out for quite a while. It will be lunch time in an hour."

They turn heading toward the house. All the way back, she can't get that word off her mind. "Die."

They spend many nights with her parents, going on outings for picnics and outdoor celebrations. The evenings alone are relaxed, with time spent among family and friends, engaged and happy. They invite his parents down for a few weeks. All too quickly the summer approaches its end. Celeste dreads leaving her parents. She wishes they could just live here, but his business is in New York. Even though he is more relaxed here, she can see his anxiety about being away from work.

"Are things okay at work, Edward?"

"Yes darling, why do you ask?"

"You seem stressed," she says laying her hand over his.

"Darling, I will always be anxious over work. That's the price you pay for owning your own business."

"You are sure everything is okay?" she says wanting him to share his thoughts with her.

"Actually, business is booming. That is what you see on my face. I have many things to attend to for the new buildings we have been hired to design. I have a great staff in New York. They keep me apprised of everything. Business has grown exponentially, so at times things can be quite demanding."

"Good. I'm glad, Edward. I know how much you love your business."

"I do, Celeste. I love what I do. I think that's why your father and I get along so well. I can discuss things with him since he was in the same business prior to retiring."

"You two do get along well. I think he respects you." She kisses him gently on the lips. "You have made his daughter very happy."

Edward looks at her. They gaze lovingly into each other's eyes. Even after all these years of marriage, just to gaze at her is a gift. He runs his finger along her cheek, bringing her chin up to kiss her. He backs away to look at her again. "The first day I saw you, I knew I would spend the rest of my life with you."

She kisses him on the lips, "I knew the first night we had dinner, you were the man I had always dreamed of. I knew my father would approve as well."

"We were destined," he starts kissing her again. He kisses her a second time teasing her again, "We need to practice making babies."

She gives him a beguiling smile. "We have been practicing a lot."

He checks his watch, then around at the empty room. "Well it's late, Catherine is asleep, and the staff has retired for the evening. I see no reason for practice not to happen now. We need practice to get it right."

She ponders his words and agrees, "Yes, we need the practice." Placing her arms around his neck, she pulls him close and whispers in his ear, "Edward, I love you more than life itself."

He pulls her in close. "I love you darling."

They go upstairs and the love between them that night is like fireworks. The touch of hand-in-hand, skin to skin, heart to heart propels them to the deepest level of love they have ever known with each other. They are frantic in their desire, but tender in their touch. Their kisses are sweet, demanding, searching, and satisfying. They enter a new level of love this night. They are truly one heart. Lying in the dark in each other's arms, appetites sated, Celeste finds emotions are exploding and tears begin to well up in her eyes. They fall down her cheek, onto Edward's chest.

He feels the wet tears on his chest. Turning his face down to hers, he inquires, "What's wrong, Celeste?"

"I am overwhelmed with love for you."

"And that makes you sad enough to cry?"

She tries to control herself from sobbing uncontrollably. "No silly, my tears are tears of joy. I have been so blessed in my life with you."

He kisses her lightly, "Honey, I am the lucky one. You could have had any man you wanted, but you chose me. I knew there was something special between us, but as the years have passed our love has exceeded all expectations. We don't just practice being husband and wife. We love being married. You have given me a beautiful daughter and, of course, we will have a son too." He smiles and kisses her and continues. "We just practiced making the son, and will continue to do that." He laughs. "When I touch you, I am alive deep down in my soul. You were born for me, Celeste, and I was born for you."

She reaches up, kisses him then repeats his words. "I was born for you, you were my destiny."

They cling to each other that night. Both fall asleep, bodies entwined together. They do not part until the sun comes up early the next morning.

They bathe and go down for breakfast at eight o'clock. Edward is spending the day with Celeste's father to discuss his business plans for a large account he has just been awarded. Edward respects Celeste's father and seeks his opinion for many aspects of this new venture. William loves his son-in-law and is eager to help. Since he retired years earlier, he has missed the satisfaction of a hard day at work.

Edward kisses Catherine and Celeste then tells them daddy will be home around four. "Don't have the staff prepare dinner. We will go out tonight with your parents. I have already discussed it with them. We only have a week left before we return to New York, so we should spend some extra time with them."

Celeste likes the idea and is agreeable with the plans. She walks him outside and kisses him before he leaves. He puts his arms around her pulling her in tight. He kisses her forehead then sweetly on the lips, hating to leave.

Edward walks backwards, looking at her standing in front of the house. He yells, "I love this place. I love you and my sweet Catherine. See you in a bit."

She laughs at his exuberant yelling. She blows an exaggerated kiss, and he pretends it almost knocks him down. She bends over holding her stomach, laughing outrageously. As she turns, entering the house, she thinks about the emotional night they had last night. She turns back to see the car disappearing around the corner. It has the man she loves behind the wheel.

She spends the day thinking about the packing that needs to be done for the return to New York. She instructs the staff to begin packing things that will not be needed during the next week. She leisurely walks the grounds and takes Catherine out for a picnic at lunch. She lies on the balcony taking in the sun's rays, relaxing before dressing for dinner. It will feel nice dressing up to go out.

The nanny puts Catherine down for a nap around two. She goes upstairs and tries to nap too, but finds she can't relax enough to sleep. She gets up to search through her clothes for a dress for the night. She selects a light weight floral dress. She decides it's the right choice, since it's a hot day. She will take a sweater if it cools off later. Laying it out on the bed, she starts downstairs when she hears a car pull up out front.

Her father bursts through the door and sees her on the staircase. Celeste can see the distress on his face. "What is it, father?"

There is no easy way to tell her, so he bursts it out. "It's Edward, Celeste. He has had a massive heart attack."

Celeste is stunned speechless. "What did you say? He had a heart attack?"

"Yes, Celeste. Come on, I need to get you to the hospital."

She looks around to see the nanny at the top of the staircase.

The nanny yells, "Go, Mrs. Harrington. I have Catherine."

Celeste runs the rest of the way down the stairs. Her father grabs her hand pulling her to the door. All the way to the hospital, she just sits there in a state of shock. Her father tells her how they were sitting outside talking about business, then without warning, Edward grabbed his chest and fell over. It happened so fast. I didn't have a clue of what was transpiring at first. They got him to the hospital quickly. "He was still alive when I left to come get you," he sighs looking over at her with worry.

Suddenly, the words came back to her, "Die." She folds her hands over her face to keep from screaming. The word keeps repeating in her brain. "Die, Die, Die."

They arrive at the hospital and are guided to the critical care unit. Edward is on a breathing apparatus. He is pale and motionless. She walks toward the bed, and is horrified at what lays in front of her. She takes his hand in hers and says, "Edward, its Celeste. Please wake up, darling. It's time to go home."

Her mother walks over to her placing her arm around her shoulder and says, "Honey, he can't hear you."

"Yes, he can. Edward, honey, wake up."

The doctor walks in and relays Edward's untimely condition. "His heart has been damaged beyond repair. He is barely alive, hanging on by a thread. There seems to be no brain function or reaction to any responsive testing. We can assume he is brain dead at this point. When they brought him in, we could barely get a pulse. I don't know what is keeping him alive at this point.

Celeste looks at her father and screams, "Daddy. This can't be happening!"

Her father rushes over to her and takes her in his arms. She breaks down. Sobbing uncontrollably, she falls to the floor. Her father, uncertain what to do, kneels and rocks her back and forth. "I am so sorry, baby."

Elizabeth is crying into her kerchief trying to keep it together for Celeste, but finds it is too overwhelming to contain. She leaves the room trying not to make it worse for Celeste.

William tells Celeste that he has already called Edward's parents. He did it before he came to get her. They are on their way.

Celeste nods her head in acknowledgement. She pulls herself up from the floor to go back over to Edward. Sliding the chair beside the bed, she sits reaching to hold his hand. The nightmare of last night flashes through her mind. She feels the loss seeping deep into her soul. "Edward, please don't leave me," she cries into his hand.

Her father feels she needs a private moment with him and leaves the room.

Celeste looks into Edward's face. She leans in to kiss his cheek. "I love you," she cries through choked tears. "You said you would never leave me, Edward." In her anger toward God she asks, "Why are you doing this to us?" Attentively, she sits holding his hand for hours. Her father and mother sit on a small couch in front of the hospital window, giving her space to grieve, but close enough for support.

The next morning arrives with the sun behind clouds. The doctor comes in at six o'clock a.m. He asks them to leave the room while he examines Edward. William and Elizabeth go out into the hallway, but Celeste insists on staying.

The doctor comes out into the hallway after examining Edward. He informs them that there is no change.

William acknowledges and lowers his head in despair. "His parents are on their way. I'd like you to talk to them when they arrive."

The doctor nods, "I understand. Have the staff contact me when they get here."

William shakes his hand. With devastation, he returns to the room. By one o'clock, twenty four hours later, Edward's parents arrive. His mother wails in anguish at the sight of her son hooked up to the tubes. His father holds her in his arms while tears roll down his face. Celeste moves away to let his mother in close to him. She goes over to her mother and father and buries her face in her dad's chest. Her heart is broken. She feels that the act of breathing is too much effort.

After a few hours, Edward's mother and Celeste hold each other and cry. The doctor stops by to check in. Edward's father and William walk out into the hallway with him. Edward's father asks, "Is there nothing we can do?"

The doctor replies, "We have double checked his stats, and he is brain dead. His heart is barely beating. I'm afraid there is nothing we can do. I'm so sorry."

Seeing Edward's father is close to breaking down, the doctor leaves, giving him the time he needs to take in the situation. Edward's father and William stay in the hallway to discuss Edward's condition. Celeste and Edward's mother are breaking down by the moments. Returning to the room, they relay the doctor's news. Celeste and both mothers are devastated at the final news. Everyone knows he won't make it, but no one has the heart to say it out loud to her. Celeste goes back to his bedside and asks to be alone with him. Everyone leaves the room while she talks to him about their life together. She tells him their love goes beyond life. She spends two hours talking to him, then crying, begging him to wake up. Finally, she knows she has to give up. The pale look on his face, the empty expression, and lack of warmth told her he was no longer there. When the parents return to the room, she tells Edward's father that there is no response. He nods his head then leaves to get the doctor.

It's late when the doctor arrives back at the hospital. Edward has been in a comatose state almost two days now. His breathing is getting raspy and sporadic. Celeste had not slept at all and is exhausted. The doctor walks slowly into the room with a priest. The priest gives blessing over Edward. Celeste holds his left hand, while his mother holds his right. It's as if Edward knows it is time. As he takes his last breath, Celeste feels the air go out of the room like a swoosh. The silence in the room is deafening. His heart stops immediately. The doctor pronounces him dead at 11:45 p.m. The room breaks out into sobs and wails of grief. Celeste feels her heart being torn from her body. Her gut wants to hurl with nausea. She begins to shake uncontrollably. Her father comes to her and holds her. She cries into his chest until she has nothing left. Her life just ended. She wants to live no more.

CHAPTER 16

LIFE WITHOUT EDWARD

The next few months are a blur to Celeste. Her father takes care of the funeral arrangements. William contacts Edward's business associates and friends in New York with the news. He arranges with the local hotels to reserve rooms for guests arriving from New York for the funeral, which will be held in Virginia. The burial plot has been approved and located on a private area at Celestial Manor. It's not in view of the house, but a half-hour walk could get anyone there easily. Directional signs are placed on the property for vehicles to follow to the grave site the day of the funeral.

Celeste says nothing. When her father asks for her preferences, she cannot answer him. "Please just take care of it father." She goes to her room to be alone. She wants no one to say Edward is dead. She lies in bed hugging his jacket, crying into the pillow. When a knock on the door sounds, she pretends to be asleep. Once the door closes, she opens her eyes. She wants this nightmare to end and let her wake up from a bad dream. Every time she opens her eyes, she pretends he will walk in the door. She breaks down with the reality that he is never coming back.

On the day of the funeral, Elizabeth approaches Celeste's bed. "Celeste, Honey. You need to get ready for the funeral."

"I can't mother. Don't ask me to do that."

"Honey, you will regret it if you don't. You were always present for Edward for his business. Do this today for him. He would want you to do that."

In that moment, she knew her mother was right. Together Celeste and Edward had been a strong team for the development of his business. They displayed a partnership for those to view in admiration. She can't let him down now. She sits up, rubbing her eyes and goes to bathe. She chooses a black, three-quarter length sleeved dress. The matching hat has a thick matching drape that falls to cover her face. With this coverage, she feels she can bear this mournful duty. She can still be alone under the hat, behind the drape.

When she arrives down stairs, the house is full of concerned well-wishers. Everyone comes to her relaying their sympathies. She nods her head to each without saying a word. The cover over her face makes her feel detached, able to hide her grief. Business associates and their wives parade through one at a time to show support. William, Elizabeth, along with Edward's parents, show outward gratitude for their presence.

"Hello, Celeste," Mr. Grayson says with a tone of despair.

She looks up quickly to see the only man that Edward had been jealous of. Adrianna was by his side.

"I'll bet you don't want the life I have now, do you Mr. Grayson?" She is stunned at her own words.

He is taken off guard as well, but understands her grief and replies, "Celeste, I am so sorry for your loss."

She nods at him. Adrianna moves in front of him to hug her. Adrianna says, "Celeste, if I can do anything for you, please let me know."

Celeste nods and returns her hug.

Attendance at the graveside service is very large. William had made the right decision to hold the funeral outside since there are so many attending. No building could hold the many supporters who came to show their respects. Chairs are stretched as far as you can see. Rows and rows circle the casket. Arriving at the grave site, William steps out of the car. He opens the door for Celeste and Elizabeth. Edward's parents are close behind. Walking down a long aisle toward the casket that looms large in front of her, she gets light headed. She feels she is going to faint and staggers. Her father grabs her tightly. Holding her, they make their way to the seats directly in front of the casket. She sits. Her head begins to pound causing nausea to creep in. She breathes deeply trying to regain composure. She had spent hours with Edward's body that morning. To think he will be put in the ground, never seeing his face again overwhelms her with grief. During the service, she has visions of their lives together. Facing a future without his love is torture. The words of consolation from the priest fall hollow in her heart. When the funeral is over, she goes back to the manor and takes refuge in her room.

Elizabeth and Edward's mother try to convince her to come down stairs to see those who have paid Edward their respects. "I can't mother. Please thank them all for coming. I need to be alone."

In the months to come, William goes to New York to handle business for Edward. Celeste is now the complete owner. William puts the business up for sale, and handles the affairs until it's sold. They offer the business to Edward's father, but he, too, has retired, and does not wish to return to fulltime work. He advises William to sell it to provide for Celeste and Catherine. Edward's investments will keep Celeste and Catherine financially secure for their lifetime.

Celeste's life now consists of sitting in silence. She stays in Virginia near her parents. The holidays are received as a side show that she does not wish to participate in. She watches her daughter laugh and giggle over the presents from Santa. She feels no joy for the first Christmas holiday without her husband. Her parents watch her and are concerned. They take Catherine home with them days at a time to allow Celeste time to heal. She spends her time huddled in her room, or walking to Edward's grave in the bitter cold.

The winter comes hard with snow measured by feet not inches. They are closed in at Celestial Manor for days while the snow refuses to let up. The fireplaces are lit, and warmth fills the house from the crackling of wood from the fire. Celeste escapes life continuing her solitude, causing great concern for her parents. "Celeste, you need to think of Catherine more than you think of Edward. She needs her mother," her father coaxes with strong conviction.

"I can't, father. I just can't be there for her right now. You and mother can watch her for me."

Elizabeth says, "Celeste, she is part of Edward. He gave you a gift of himself. Love the gift as you did him."

The words shake Celeste. "Catherine is part of Edward" keeps reeling in her head. She sees Catherine playing with her doll. She studies the facial features of a child who has a great deal of her father's looks. "You're right," she admits getting up to walk over to Catherine. "She is a gift that he gave us."

As she starts toward Catherine, Celeste finds she's not steady on her feet. She loses balance and stumbles to the couch. William rushes over to her as she loses consciousness. He carries her upstairs to her room while Elizabeth calls the doctor. Hours later, after the doctor's visit, they are told she is undernourished. Acknowledging that they knew she rarely ate, they asked for help from the doctor.

He replies, "I think she needs emotional therapy to help deal with the loss of her husband." He recommends a therapist and a nutritional menu that should assist in her recovery.

The next day, William has Dr. Hirschman, an emotional therapist at the house by ten in the morning.

The therapist collects the history of the situation from William and Elizabeth and then goes to Celeste's room. Elizabeth escorts him in, introducing him. Celeste looks at her mother's stern face and realizes there is no use in trying to argue, so she decides to endure the meeting.

Shaking his hand, Celeste motions toward the two chairs in front of the fireplace. Elizabeth leaves the room closing the door lightly.

He begins slowly, "Celeste, your parents have filled me in on your husband's death. They have shared the impact that it has had on you. Can you share some of your feelings with me about his death?"

She sits staring at the sparkling fire and doesn't reply. The heaviness in her body consumes her at the thought of speaking of losing Edward. To say it out loud would crush her, or consume her to lose all the strength she has left in her.

"Take your time, there's no pressure. I have heard from your parents of your devastating loss. I was hoping to hear it in your words," he silently waits for a response.

She lowers her head to the handkerchief she holds in her hand. Gradually the words begin, "I cannot live without him."

Dr. Hirschman replies, "What about your daughter? Does she not give you a reason to live?"

She sits silently playing with the kerchief. "She is a reminder of him. It is difficult for me to look at her."

He replies, "I can see that it would be difficult for you. Do you think you could ever see her as a piece of your husband that should be treasured? He loved you so much that he gave you a part of him. No other woman can say that."

With tears streaming from her eyes, she nods yes. "He was so happy when we found out I was pregnant."

"Then he would expect you to take care of the gift he gave you. She should be your reason for living, and moving on from this tragedy," he says reaching over to lay his hand on her trembling shoulder as she releases the pain through tears. He sits in silence while she covers her face with the kerchief releasing the sobs that she has long needed to let go of.

Pulling herself together, she slowly relays her thoughts to Dr. Hirschman. "I feel anger at Edward for leaving us. I feel pain every time I look at my daughter because she looks so much like him. I feel lost in life not knowing what to do without him. My life was built around Edward. Our days were built around his life. The business, formal dinners, the galas and his love were everything. Without those, what is my purpose?" She seeks a response from him. Knowing his next statement by the expression on his face, she says, "Before you say it, I know I have Catherine. That is not what I mean. Edward and I together had purpose. We worked hard, planning every step of our lives. We made investments in our future." Examining the room, she says, "We built this place so that I could be close to my family and we could retire here when he was ready. Everything is gone, just like that!"

Dr. Hirschman replies, "You have every right to be angry."

She looks at him surprised at the reply. She thought he would admonish her for her selfishness. She says nothing.

"You had your whole life planned out. He was in the center of those plans. No wonder you are lost now. When we lose loved ones, there is despair, anger, and depression, before acceptance.

You have been through the first three, but failed to enter acceptance."

"I don't want to accept it. I can't!"

"Celeste, you have no choice. Edward is gone. You have to decide not to waste everything Edward provided for your future. He sacrificed greatly to give you the life you have. He would be sad to see you throwing away everything he worked for. It would hurt him to know your feelings toward your daughter because she looks like him. He would want you to be happy that you see him in her. He left a gift of himself. Will you throw away a life that he provided for you?"

Celeste stares at Dr. Hirschman stunned at his frank words.

"You're right. I know you are, but how do I lose the sadness?"

He replies, "One day at a time. Take one step at a time to embrace life again. It won't happen overnight, but you must make the effort to get there." He scrutinizes her and sees a face that is so contorted in sadness. He leans toward her and softly says, "One day at a time, okay?"

She smiles at him and says, "I'll try."

"That is all anyone can ask. Edward will be smiling."

She looks into his sympathetic eyes and repeats, "One day at a time."

He stands to leave, and she gets up to see him to the door. "Would you like to take the first step and join your family down stairs?"

Hesitantly, she agrees, "Okay, I can try."

He can see she is fragile, so he offers his arm to her and they proceed downstairs.

William and Elizabeth are surprised to see her come down with him but are elated that she has. Her mother quickly picks up the throw on the large chair assisting her to be seated. Her father glances toward the therapist, with hopeful encouragement.

Dr. Hirschman states, "Celeste, it was a pleasure meeting you." He turns to Elizabeth and says the same. He turns to leave. William quickly steps beside him to escort him out.

Out of hearing range, Dr. Hirschman tells William that he has high-hopes that she will turn a corner now. He will return on

Thursday to check in on how she is doing, and plans to continue with her counseling if they approve.

William nods, "Absolutely. Please do come, Dr. Hirschman."

He closes the door behind Dr. Hirschman. Returning to the room, he sees Catherine sitting in the chair beside Celeste. Celeste is running her hands through Catherine's hair, while having a mother-daughter talk about her doll. He looks at Elizabeth, who is almost in tears with happiness of the affection Celeste is showing her daughter. He walks to Elizabeth putting his arms around her and says, "We should have taken the counseling step much sooner."

Elizabeth smiles and nods in agreement.

That night, Celeste has dinner with the family, engaging in plans for the next few days. The change in Celeste is nothing outside of a miracle. She is laughing, talking and has a new, more peaceful expression on her face. At bedtime, she tucks in Catherine, and reads her a bedtime story. Kissing Catherine goodnight, Elizabeth, William, and Celeste each retire to their rooms. Celeste bathes and sits in front of the fireplace thinking about what Dr. Hirschman had said earlier. A knock on her door sounds, disturbing her out of her thoughts of tomorrow.

William and Elizabeth walk in, to say goodnight. They both kiss her telling her it was wonderful having her down stairs tonight.

Celeste sadly says, "Mom, Dad, I'm so sorry I have been such a mess since Edward's death. I know you tried to help me, but I wasn't ready to hear it. I am now. Dr. Hirschman said Edward would not be happy if I lived a life he had planned for us without acceptance. When I now think about it, maybe Catherine is what he gave me to help me survive this loss. Instead of the pain that seeing her was doing to me, I should embrace the gift."

William bent down and kissed her on the head. Almost losing composure, he smiles, "Let us help you into bed, Celeste. You had more activity today than you have had in a long while. You look weak."

Agreeing, Celeste stands up between William and Elizabeth. The three walk to the bed. She sheds her robe and climbs in. With kisses and good nights, her mother and father leave the room relieved that Celeste is finally returning to herself again. They have renewed hope for her recovery. Both sleep better than they have in quite a while.

During the night, Celeste wakes clutching her chest. She has pain in her neck, chest, and shooting down her left arm. Trying to get up, she finds she has no strength to do so. She lay there realizing with torment, that she is having a heart attack. A sudden pain shoots through her chest again. She is forced up from pain ravishing her chest. As she lies there in the dark, she sees Edward standing over her bed.

Edward speaks to her, "It's okay, my love, I'm here."

She gets excited. Her heart begins to pound rapidly. She finds it hard to get her breath. She looks at Edward and says, "I'm scared."

"Don't be afraid, my love. I'm here waiting for you."

Celeste watches Edward bend, kissing her on the lips. Her heart fills with emotion, and tears of joy spill from her eyes. The realization that she is going to be with Edward allows her to let go. Her last thought before moving to the other side is of Catherine.

Edward assures her they will be there for her. With this, she let's go and crosses over to death.

Instead of Edward being there, she is standing in her room alone. Looking at the bed, she sees herself lying there understanding that she is now dead. Distraught she turns around searching for Edward, but he's not there. A vibrant light begins to glow from the ceiling. It fills the room with brightness she has never seen. She feels the light beckoning for her to come towards it. She searches again for Edward, but she can't see him. Turning from the light, she frantically screams for Edward. She stares back at the light and yells, "I can't leave without Edward. He's here. I just saw him." The light begins to dim slowly. It doesn't completely disappear, as if trying to coax her to come to the light. She moves towards the light and it brightens again, inviting her to accept it. Each time she turns away to search for Edward, it dims darker. Suddenly, the light vanishes and she is alone with her dead body. She begins to cry hysterically. "Where are you, Edward? Where are you?"

At daybreak, she sits on the chair in front of the fireplace. Her dead body solemnly lays there, now a pale white corpse. She views the image of herself. She did not realize before how skinny she has gotten. The frail body before her was unrecognizable. She has aged, evident by the loose and wrinkled skin on her face. Her hands were skeletal with traces of bone pronounced.

At eight o'clock, the door opens to her room. Elizabeth enters the room. She sees Celeste's non-breathing pale body, grasping the horrible situation immediately. She screams, running from the room yelling for William. William enters the room running past Elizabeth and takes in the sight of his daughter. Losing all control, he cries fiercely over her body.

Celeste watches in horror. She sees the pain in her parent's faces, and feels uncontrolled despair. She watches as the maid enters the room. William yells for her to call the doctor.

The maid leaves the room. William and Elizabeth sit beside Celeste's fragile unmoving body. They weep for the loss of their only daughter. As the undertaker removes Celeste's body from the house, sobs echo throughout. The doctor tells them that malnutrition may have damaged the heart, causing a heart attack. They will know after the autopsy.

William says sadly, "I think she died of a broken heart."

Celeste watches while her physical body is removed from the house. Seeing her parents in so much despair is difficult. For days the house is in turmoil. The devastation of Celeste's death is felt throughout the community, and New York. All are shocked at the news. After the funeral where she is laid beside Edward, William and Elizabeth decide to take Catherine home with them. On the day of their departure, Celeste follows her mother into Catherine's room. Elizabeth packs her grand-daughter's belongings into cases. William arrives just as Elizabeth has packed the final items. He takes the bags, and they leave Celestial Manor. Celeste wants to follow them, but feels she can't get close to the door.

After the door closes, she runs back upstairs intent on finding Edward. She runs from room to room searching for him. Calling his name repeatedly, she waits for a response. Everyone has left, even the staff that lived with her. Silence is all she hears now.

Day after day, Celeste roams the halls of Celestial Manor, grief stricken that she has lost everyone. Her family no longer comes back to the house. She is unable to find Edward. She has never felt so alone. Her sadness is all that keeps her company now.

William and Elizabeth contact Edward's parents to discuss decisions about the estate. They discuss what should happen with Catherine. Both families agree she would be better off with Celeste's parents. The Harrington's make plans to regularly visit Virginia to see her. Their plans include taking her to New York as well. Everyone operates with the consensus of what is best for the child. The grand-child is showered with an abundance of love.

As the years go by, Catherine grows into a beautiful young lady. She has the elegance and beauty of her parents, and the attributes of Edward's brilliant mind. Making trips to stay with Edward's parents provides great connections in New York. She remains in Virginia with William and Elizabeth, making her life there. Catherine decides, after leaving Celestial Manor empty for years to sell it. Edward planned well for the family, so Catherine never has to work a day in her life if she doesn't wish to.

Catherine meets, and marries Douglas Turner at the age of twenty two. They have a son named Brandon Turner. He marries Sophia and out of that union, Megan (Bridgette's mother) is born in 1965. Catherine dies at the age of seventy four from heart failure. Megan meets Derek Chandler and marries him in 1991 at the age of 26. They have Bridgette in 1993. Unfortunately Megan's life comes to a tragic end in an automobile accident in 2005, when Bridgette is only 12 years of age.

CHAPTER 17

RETURN TO REALITY

Bridgette returns to her own life in a state of confusion. Having been in a coma for over 24 hours, she wakes to a new reality and soon finds that she has experienced a miracle. She has traveled across time to the past to know and feel two hearts that were not her own.

The nurse is doing a routine exam, checking Bridgette's pulse, temperature and IV drip. Once all vitals are checked, the nurse leaves the room. Minutes after her departure, Bridgette's father stops by to check on her. Bridgette has been unresponsive. His medical background provides no insight of what has happened to his daughter. No doctor has been able to explain the reason for her mysterious state. As Dr. Chandler kisses the top of her head, she moves slightly. With excitement in his voice he says, "Bridgette, can you hear me?"

Bridgette hears something in the distance, but can't make out what it is. She hears mumbles and garbled sounds that are not discernable. She moans.

Dr. Chandler pulls off his stethoscope to listen to her heart. He checks her pulse for rapid response. "Honey, can you hear me?"

Eyes closed, deliriously, she moans, "Dad?"

"Yes, honey it's me."

"Dad, what's going on? My head hurts."

"You're in the hospital."

Her thinking is fuzzy. Eyes still closed, she tries to remember what happened, for her to be hospitalized. She can't remember anything. As hard as she tries to think, nothing comes to her.

Seeing her struggle her father advises, "Bridgette, just relax. Everything will come back to you later. You don't have to figure this out now."

Gradually, she opens her eyes. At first, her sight is blurred. It slowly clears as she surveys the hospital room. She asks, "Dad, why am I in the hospital?"

Her father is careful with his reply not wishing to upset her. "Honey, we don't know what happened to you. You fainted, and an ambulance was called. We have completed some tests, but nothing has shown up on the scans to explain why you fainted."

She asks, "How long have I been out?"

"Over twenty-four hours," he says evenly, trying not to upset her.

She sits up in bed, feeling weak and groggy still. "Can I go home?"

"Honey, now that you're awake, I want to order some cognizant testing to make sure nothing is wrong. Do you think you could bear with me, to get these tests?"

"Sure dad."

Her father asks, "What is the last thing you remember?"

She tries to recall what she was doing, but nothing comes. "I can't remember, dad. Let me think about it a bit. I feel confused, somewhat disoriented."

He replies, "Okay honey, just rest for a while. We'll talk later. I'm going to get some food sent up to you now. Food should help with your weakness."

"Okay dad."

He kisses her on the head. Leaving the room, he pulls out his phone to make some calls to cancel his rounds and appointments for the evening. He orders the tests he wants. He will spend some time with her to evaluate her state of mind. For now, he chooses not to discuss what happened to her at Celestial Manor. It may bring everything back, but he doesn't want to stress her.

Not long after he leaves the room, a hospital tray with food arrives. Celeste lifts the lid to see a nice meal. While she is still holding the lid, her father walks back in. "It smells great Dad. I just realized I'm starving." She smiles at him with exaggerated enthusiasm.

Her father grins as he takes the lid from her and lays it on one of the empty chairs. This is good news. He still feels uneasy though, not having answers to her fainting and comatose state. He says, "Eat up." Bridgette eats with no sign of nausea or symptoms of illness. It comforts him to see she has an appetite. He decides to sit with her until the hospital staff arrives to take her for the ordered tests. Looking at his watch, he realizes it's late. He stands to move the tray from in front of her, commenting that she didn't clean her plate.

"Dad, now don't start getting over sensitive. When have you ever seen me clean my plate?"

He smiles at her, nodding acknowledgement. "I'm just worried about you, honey. We don't know what caused your collapse. Bear with your old man's concerns."

"I know, dad. I understand. It puzzles me, too." Smiling at her concerned dad, an attendee arrives to wheel Bridgette out of the room for tests. She returns and is back in her room in less than an hour. She feels satisfied she has met her father's demands. Her plan is to go home if nothing shows up.

It was as if her father was a mind reader. He is in her room only minutes after she returns. He had gotten the call that the tests were complete. Before he goes to check them out, he wants to settle her in for the night. "Get some rest, honey. I'll be by first thing in the morning before I make rounds."

Feeling tired, she responds, "Can you make it after rounds? Dad, before rounds is way too early."

He laughs. "Okay, after rounds then. See you in the morning." He checks her vitals one last time and then leaves, deciding on the way out of her room to review her tests, and check on some of his critical patients.

She pushes the button to lower her bed. In a half upright position, she reviews in her mind what has occurred the last 24 hours. Feeling drowsy, she lowers her bed the rest of the way. Soon, she is sleeping fitfully.

In her dreams, Celeste comes to her. "Bridgette, don't forget me. I need you to remember."

Bridgette's mind begins to replay what she saw during her comatose state during the last 24 hours. Everything comes flooding back. Celeste, Edward, and Catherine become clear to her now. Celeste tells her not to be afraid. Bridgette jumps awake. Sitting up with a pounding heart, she recalls her dream. She is all too aware of what had occurred to her now. She remembers Celeste charging toward her when she collapsed.

It's the middle of the night, but she lays there in the darkness remembering everything Celeste revealed to her. Trying to shake the fear, she knows that Celeste needs her. She decides there is nothing left to do but help her. She needs to decide who she can trust to share this with. Some will think she has lost her mind, or that she's crazy. Her father would protest without hesitation. Telling her father would be a mistake. Her next thought is of Jason. He knew she was going there that day to see Celeste. Heck, he saw her himself. He would understand before anyone else would.

The next morning, she rises early. Taking a shower, she puts on the clothes that are hanging in the wardrobe closet. She's sitting on the chair, waiting for her father to come by later in the morning. She wants to get checked out of the hospital. She speaks to her doctor on his rounds and asks about checking out, but he says he would need to speak with her father before releasing her. He thought her father wanted to keep her a day or so for observation.

At eleven, Jason walks in.

She is surprised, "Jason. Hi, how are you? How did you know I was in the hospital?"

"Victor called informing me of your situation. Having found you in Celeste's room unconscious, he was concerned and wanted to know if I had heard anything about you. He had tried your number at home with no success in reaching you. How are you?"

"I feel fine," she informs him, still surprised that he has come to see her.

Moments later, her father walks in. He says, holding out his hand to Jason to shake it, "Hello, Jason. It's good to see you again."

Bridgette looks at the two, "You two know each other?"

Dr. Chandler replies, "He came by yesterday to check on you, I met him then. He told me about you two meeting at Celestial Manor."

"Oh." She looks at him thinking it was a lovely gesture of Jason to come by two days in a row. "Thank you for coming by Jason. That was thoughtful of you."

He replies, "No problem. I was concerned when Victor called me. I wish I had gone with you."

She realizes rather quickly that he is about to discuss the ghost, so she abruptly jumps in with an interruption to deter the conversation. "It was nice of you to come here two days in a row. I know you must be busy at work. Dad, Jason is a local architect."

Dr. Chandler asks, "Architect?" He looks at Jason and says, "There are tons of old historical buildings in this area. Are you into historical or modern designs?"

Jason looks at Bridgette before responding to Dr. Chandler. He sees the pleading in her eyes not to talk about the ghost. He replies to Dr. Chandler, "I like both actually. I love the history of this city. My professional designs are more modern buildings. Have you heard of the Cardigan building? That's one of my designs."

Dr. Chandler replies, "You're kidding? That building is beautiful. Looking at Bridgette, he says, his designs are very high scale."

Jason smiles, "Thank you, Dr. Chandler. I'm very proud of that one. Actually, that's how I met Bridgette. I visited Celestial Manor with peaked interest in the historical design for my next project. Your daughter and I won a prize drawn from the open house. We met during a private luncheon award."

Dr. Chandler watches Bridgette with curiosity. She has not mentioned this specifically to him. Dr. Chandler inquires of Jason, "Did she tell you that her great, great grand-parents owned it at one point?"

Jason nods, "Yes, we did talk about that. She looks inordinately like her great, great grandmother. You couldn't miss the resemblance."

Bridgette breaks the conversation with, "Dad, would you please authorize my admitting doctor to release me?"

"Honey, I'd like to keep you a day or two for observation," he replies with his doctor-advising voice. "Your tests didn't show anything, so that leaves me concerned."

"Dad, I will go stir crazy if I don't get out of here. There's nothing wrong with me. I feel fine."

"I'm not sending you home alone, Bridgette. I have to work this evening, so I won't be available to check on you." He's making excuses not to release her.

Jason intervenes with, "Dr. Chandler, I'd be happy to spend the evening with Bridgette until you get off. I can take her dinner, and stay until you're free."

Dr. Chandler hesitates, "Thanks, Jason. I wouldn't let her go otherwise." Looking back at her he says, "With better judgment, I should say no, but okay. You will not lift one finger to do anything. Is that clear?"

She beams that knowing smile that wraps him around her little finger. "Yes dad, that's fine." She gives Jason a smile of gratitude for the help in convincing her father.

Jason says, "Well, let me get out of here and get to work. They exchange numbers, and he says he will call her if he has any questions. He will need to go home to shower, and with the decision to bring take-out food, time to pick it up. "Does seven sound okay?"

She replies, "Seven o'clock is perfect."

Jason says, "Okay, see you later," he tells her father good-by then turns and leaves.

She gets checked out just in time for her father to take her home. She has eaten a bite for lunch provided by the hospital, so she needs nothing. With Jason coming by later, she decides to take her father's advice and relax.

Her father kisses her forehead before heading out the door. "Call me if you need anything. I'll see you later." The door closes behind him.

She looks for the remote. Lying back on the couch, she closes her eyes, taking her father's advice. She naps on and off all evening. Feeling a little drained, she settles in. Around six she wakes up and takes a shower. She admits to herself, Jason coming by excites her. She is extra attentive with her makeup and hair.

She smiles at her reflection in the mirror with giddy nerves. Trying to decide the exact outfit becomes daunting. Nothing she puts on, suites her mood. After trying on six different outfits, she decides on a short-sleeve white blouse and a pair of jean shorts. The casual outfit compliments her tan, deepening the gray blue of her eyes. Emphasizing her long lashes with the dark mascara gives her a seductive appeal.

At seven on the dot, her door-bell rings. She takes her time before opening the door. She doesn't want to seem too anxious. When she pulls the door open, her heart skips a beat. His dark handsome face and smile is captivating. His eyes are as blue as the sky. His dress is casual with jeans and a light weight, short-sleeve white shirt. She backs up to let him in the door. He's carrying a bag of food from her favorite restaurant. She can smell the pasta as he walks past her. "That smells delicious."

He agrees, "I love this restaurant. I purchased salads, pastas, and desserts. I wanted to make sure I had whatever you'd like."

Smelling the aromas again, she says, "You are successful, everything smells so good." She pushes her phone and books aside on the coffee table to make room for the food. "Do you mind eating here, or would you rather eat at the table?"

He sets the bag on the coffee table, "Here's fine."

They sit for a bit before eating to discuss her test results. "Dad says the tests show nothing, so I guess I have a clean bill of health."

"It doesn't concern you that you were in a coma for over 24 hours?"

"Of course, it concerns me, but I know the reason. You are going to think I've lost my mind, but I need to tell someone." She starts with the day of the event, the episode that sends her into the coma. Relaying a short version of the story that Celeste shared with her, she looks at Jason at the end of the tale with questioning eyes. "You think I'm crazy right?"

He sits stunned at first. "Wow. That is out of this world! Do you think the whole time it was Celeste leading you in this dream?"

"That's just it, Jason. It wasn't a dream. It was as if I was Celeste in the flesh living her life. I knew her every emotion. I knew her love for Edward and the intensity of their relationship. I could see the love in his eyes for her. I felt her heartbreak when he died. It was tangible, Jason. As clearly as I sit here before you now, it was just as real."

He hesitates, "I don't know why I'm saying this, but after seeing her myself at the manor, I believe you. I could see the pain in her face when she appeared before me. Everything in your story relates to the sadness I saw in her."

"Thank God! I was afraid you would think me insane. I'm struggling with it myself. She's asking me for help, but I don't know how to help her."

Jason sits back thoughtfully on the couch. He sees the concern on her face then says, "Look, let's review the facts. I saw Celeste, so I know what you are saying is real. Victor and Mr. Barclay saw her as well. Your vision of her life fits, with what I have studied. It is very close to real-life historical facts. You now have the decision to choose what to do about it."

"Jason, what can I do about it? She's dead. I haven't seen any ghosts of Edward, so getting them together again is not in the realm of possibilities. I certainly won't do a séance. That would completely freak me out."

Jason agrees, "I get it. I don't blame you. This is by far out of the norm, so who would know what to do? Not me, that's for sure."

She does feel a sense of calm that Jason isn't staring at her like she's a freak. He believes her. This is exactly what she was hoping for. "I guess I need to go see her again."

Jason replies without a second thought, "Not without me, you're not."

"Honestly, I think she has accomplished what she wants with me. She wanted me to know their love. I know that now. I don't think she will embody me again."

He doesn't entirely agree with that. "Maybe not, but we can't be sure of anything. Neither of us knows her intent."

"I agree," she says supporting his thoughts. "I need to help her, Jason. I need to."

"Okay, but let's make sure you are healthy first. The both of us need to be strong to confront this head on."

She replies, "I again agree." With that, she reaches for the food. They place everything out on the large coffee table, making their selections.

The phone rings around nine. It's her father. "Hi honey, I'm leaving the hospital now, need anything?"

She pauses, then answers with, "No, we just had dinner, so I'm fine."

"Okay, I will see you shortly. Tell Jason thanks for sitting with you until I arrive."

Bridgette hangs up the phone and informs Jason, "Well, he's on his way. I really appreciate you coming over Jason. I wouldn't admit this to my father, but I am still feeling a little weak so you being here comforted me."

Jason stands and bends over to pick up his keys from the coffee table. "Hey, I really enjoyed a laid back evening. The conversation was interesting, and I filled my belly. I call that a successful night." He rubs his stomach in an exaggerated motion of being full. He turns toward the door and she follows behind him. He doesn't hang around too much at the door, trying not to make leaving an awkward moment. He is so attracted to her. He looks at her full luscious lips and wonders what it would be like to kiss them.

She thanks Jason again for coming over. "Please call me when you get some time. We can decide what we need to do about Celeste. I really appreciate you wanting to help me and be a part of this."

"No problem, Bridgette. I don't want you doing this alone." He opens the door and turns to walk out. He says, "Good night, Bridgette."

"Good night, Jason.

On Jason's drive home, he reviews the evening and the information Bridgette shared with him about Celeste and Edward. He thinks to himself, "Man what a love story Celeste and Edward's life was. It is so rare to love that deeply. He thinks about all the women he has dated, and cannot remember one woman that has brought him anywhere close to those emotions." His mind moves to Bridgette. She is so beautiful. Her petite slender body looks so delicate and fragile, yet the depth of her personality provides a picture of strength. She has his mind in a state of confusion, something no woman has ever done to him. During their closeness tonight, he could smell her perfume. He kept staring at those luscious lips and gray blue eyes all night. Why is he so smitten?

Bridgette has just washed off her makeup when her father arrives. She kisses him and thanks him for coming over. He sees she looks tired and suggests she turn in. "I think I will dad. See you tomorrow?"

"I have rounds at the break of dawn tomorrow. Do you want me to wake you before I leave?"

She gives him a smile and crooks an eyebrow up then responds, "No, I think I'll pass on that."

He laughs giving an understanding nod. "Sweet dreams honey, good night."

"Night, dad."

CHAPTER 18

CONFUSED LOVE

Arriving home, Jason opens the door and throws his keys in the glass bowl on the entry table. Feeling tired, he takes a shower and settles in for the night. Looking through some of the material for work tomorrow, he soon gets drowsy. Laying the material on his night stand, he turns out the light. He is asleep before his head hits the pillow.

His dreams are about Bridgette, but with a twist. He sees Bridgette in the dream, but he is using the name Celeste when speaking to her. He walks up the wide staircase to meet her as she begins descending. He takes her hand in his and walks her down to the landing. She has on a long dress that he remembers is in one of Celeste's pictures. She's beautiful. The love he feels for her is flooding his heart. He is dazzled by her. She is so real to him. Somehow he knows this is a dream, but at the same time his feelings are so intense. The touch of her hand in his is warm. They leave the house hand in hand. Walking through the maze of flowers and fountains, they talk endlessly about nothing. Yet every time she says something it is as if she had just said she loved him. His excitement of her nearness is tantalizing his senses. The smell of her perfume is sweet and draws him in close to her. When her gray blue eyes gaze deeply into his, the world disappears. He brings her hand to his lips and kisses it. Her laugh is sweet and she affectionately pulls him close. Her full lips meet his softly with a peck.

"Edward, you are so sweet."

"Why are you calling me Edward?"

She ignores his question and keeps talking as if he has said nothing. He grabs her arm to stop walking, "Celeste, my name is Jason. You do know that right?"

"Of course I know your name. Come on, Edward. Let's go down by the lake." She turns away from him grabbing his hand to pull him toward the lake.

He follows, all the while thinking, "She called me Edward again." He dismisses the fact that he just called her Celeste, too. His thoughts return to focus on what she is saying.

She wears a happy expression on her face and holds his hand in hers. She says, "I'm told we will spend the rest of our lives together."

Confused he asks, "Who told you that?"

Something jolts him awake. He lies in the dark pondering what the dream means. "Why did I have to wake up now? She was about to tell me who told her we would be together for the rest of our lives." In the darkness of his room, he thinks about Bridgette. No woman has ever captivated him like this one. He is uncertain whether it is the situation with Celeste, or his own emotions. Of course he knows his attraction to her. She is a stunning woman. Any man would be attracted, but he has had many attractive women, so why is this one holding him captive? He can't get her out of his brain even when he sleeps. It's driving him crazy.

The next morning Bridgette is having a cup of coffee when her phone rings. It's Jason. "Bridgette, I had the craziest dream last night."

"Oh my God, I did too," shocked that he is telling her this. "What was your dream about?"

He tells her what occurred in the dream and she goes silent. "Bridgette?"

"Jason, I dreamt the same thing."

He is blown away. "You are kidding me?"

"No, Jason. I'm not."

"Bridgette, this is getting crazy. Did you go back and forth about names? I mean one minute I am Jason, then, I am Edward. I am calling you Celeste, but I see you."

"The same here," she says not believing what she is hearing.

He asks, "Do you want to meet for lunch today?"

"Sure, I'm still out of school through the rest of this week. I'll pack us a lunch and meet you at the park near your office."

"That sounds great. See you then."

Before he realizes the morning has passed, it's lunch time. Jason arrives to find Bridgette has set up a folding table, topped with plenty of food.

He laughs. "Are you feeding an army?"

She smiles, "I didn't know what kind of appetite you would have, so I came prepared."

He sits on one of the matching chairs across from her. "Man, this smells good. Did you cook it or pick it up?"

"I cooked it. I have talents," she grins.

He stares at her full lips as she smiles and responds, "I can see that." He lays his chin on his fisted knuckles and watches her. As usual, she is impeccably dressed. Her long legs, showing below the sundress, are tanned and smooth. He compares her to the dream last night. When she smiles, her gray blue eyes smile too. He decides at that moment his attraction has nothing to do with Celeste and Edward.

Bridgette is unpacking the food as she talks to him about her dream. While they eat, both relay back and forth what they saw in the dream. To their surprise, all details are identical. She looks at Jason, "I don't know what to say Jason. I'm sorry I dragged you into all of this."

"Actually, this has been the most excitement I have had in my life for a while. I'm fascinated."

She scans his handsome face, "Really? You don't think this is a little crazy?"

He laughs, "Well, I didn't say it wasn't crazy, but I think this goes beyond Celeste and Edward. You and I were chosen. What our role will be in this is yet to be seen, but I have come to care enough about Celeste and Edward to want to stick it out. Working with you in the process is not so bad either." He raises one eye brow and gives her a grin.

"Well, I guess I will tough it out having to deal with you." The breeze picks up and the napkins begin to blow. Both of them jump up and grab them at the same time. Their hands both lay on the same pile together. They look up at each other as their hands touch and pause. If electricity between two people could be seen, it would be shooting in every direction.

Feeling his touch and the pause between them is exciting. Looking into his blue eyes she nervously asks, "I hate to say it, but shouldn't you be getting back to work?"

He asks, "What are your plans for the day?"

"I don't have any at the moment."

"Care to spend it with a guy who is playing hooky from work?"

"Well, I guess I could make the sacrifice."

"Good answer," he says with a big smile.

They pack up her car with the cooler and containers of leftover food. For the rest of the day, they walk the river beside the park. They lay out a blanket under a shade tree and talk. Each gives many details about their lives. Stretching out on the blanket, she lays on her back taking in the sky. His shadow moves over her, making them face to face. Hoping he is not being too forward, he rubs his finger along her jaw line and says, "God, you're beautiful."

Her heart jumps at his statement. She instantly recognizes the emotions Celeste felt for Edward. She smiles up at him and places her hand on the back of his hand and turns her face into his hand and kisses his palm.

With this movement of acceptance, he lies on his elbow and leans in for a kiss. Their lips meet softly, lingering. He pulls away to look at her. Her eyes open slightly. They close again as he leans in for another kiss. His kiss is sweet and tender. No demands, just remaining long enough to make his heart skip a beat.

She is taken in with every movement of his lips on hers. His tenderness is making her want more of him. Her lips meet his with the same sweetness he gives. After a few minutes, they stop.

"Bridgette, this has nothing to do with Celeste and Edward. I'm very attracted to you." He takes his hand and places it behind her neck and pulls her back in for another sweet kiss.

She responds, "I'm attracted to you too, Jason." Her heart is speaking louder than her voice. It's racing.

Jason asks, "What do you say we see where this goes? Are you available to date?"

She looks at him, "I'm not seeing anyone if that's your question."

He smiles replying, "Yes, that would be my question."

They move into a sitting position with her back leaning against his chest. He wraps his arms around her waist as they watch the birds, and talk. They watch the sun set over the river and make it to their cars just before dark envelops them. Leaning her back against her car, he kisses her deeply. She responds with equal passion into the kiss. The kisses speak of a promise of tomorrow that both want. She feels at peace in his arms. He feels excitement about his future for the first time in his life. She puts her arms around his neck and gives in to his closeness.

Suddenly they hear, "Get a room."

They both laugh. Pulling apart, they realize they were really getting into the kissing. Jason says to the passerby, "Yeah, yeah." He opens the door for her. She gets in and he bends in for one more kiss. "Good night."

She runs her fingers down his jaw and kisses his lips lightly one more time. "Good night."

The two spend several weeks getting to know one another and enjoy each other's company. They even go to a movie, holding hands like two teenagers, kissing intermittently. In only a short time, they feel like they have known each other forever.

A few mornings later, Bridgette decides she wants to invite her father over for lunch. She wants to tell him about the new direction of her relationship with Jason. She's on cloud nine and can't wait to share the good news.

It's around ten o'clock when her father calls, informing her that he may not make it. "I'm sorry honey. I know you were going to a lot of trouble to fix lunch. I called Jason, to see if he could come by instead."

"You did what? Dad, I am not a child. Why would you call Jason? That's embarrassing."

"It's too soon for you to be alone, honey. I'm sorry, but we still need to keep a watchful eye on you." This has nothing whatsoever to do with her health now, he is playing matchmaker. He really likes Jason and hopes their relationship becomes more than just friends.

Dr. Chandler had said to Jason, "Jason, I have been called in for emergency surgery. I know this is a lot to ask, but is there any way you could make it to Bridgette's for lunch?"

Jason replies, "Sure, Dr. Chandler. No problem. What time should I be there?"

Dr. Chandler says, "Around one is when I told her I would arrive. Honestly, I wouldn't ask if this were not important. I know I'm being an over protective father."

Jason pauses knowing very well what he is up to, but without further hesitation accepts, "Sure, Dr. Chandler, I'd be glad to go."

Dr. Chandler, feeling proud of his success says, "Thanks Jason, I really appreciate this. She will probably insist this is not necessary, but I know she went to a lot of trouble preparing lunch, so stand firm with her about staying if she tries to dismiss your visit."

"Absolutely, I understand." Jason knows exactly what her father is up to. He is trying to be matchmaker. Her father has no clue she was going to tell him how involved they have become.

When Jason shows up on her doorstep instead of her father, she has to laugh. Her father is busted with the matchmaking scheme! She apologizes to Jason, but is glad to see him. Even though they had been together just last night, she has missed him.

Her father calls around two. While she is talking to her father, Jason puts the dishes in the dishwasher. When he returns, she has hung up from the call.

"Jason, I'm sorry my father put you on the spot. He had no right to do that."

He provides a comforting smile, "Your father knew you would say that, but it's not up for debate. I'm here, accept it." Getting ready to do a rebuttal, he silences her by placing his finger over her lips.

Removing his finger she says, "Okay. Thank you, Jason. I do appreciate your company."

He goes to the living room and relaxes on the couch. Shrugging his shoulders, he acts like the whole thing is no big deal. They sit together snuggled as they watch TV. Without realizing it, both fall fast asleep, waking up later close to sunset. It's eight o'clock.

She says, "Oh my, we slept half the day away."

Jason snuggles in and says, "It's Friday night. I don't have to work tomorrow. Do you have any plans?"

"No, nothing," she smiles. "You're okay to stay longer?"

"I have never complained about spending the evening with a beautiful woman before, I won't start now."

She thinks there it is, the first trace of flirting today. "Oh, I see how this must be a great sacrifice for you. I know it will be hard to refrain myself from taking advantage of your good graces."

He laughs out loud.

She watches his dimples deepen as his grin. She is so attracted to him. Those blue eyes would melt away the coldest heart. The last few weeks have been wonderful. Her heart is opening up to this man that she barely knows, but she is experiencing newness in her life that feels real.

Jason feels very comfortable making the decision to stay. She's beautiful. She can seduce him without even trying. Her thick long lashes and seductive gray blue eyes are piercing his soul each minute they are together. Restraining all of these weeks from taking her in his arms has been torture. Small moments of sweet kisses, has lit a flame within his heart. Her closeness is all he thinks about.

She sits beside him on the couch. Relaxing, she lays her head back on the sofa to rest. She turns her head in his direction glancing over at him as he bursts out laughing at something on the TV.

He notices her face turning toward him. He glances at her and sees something in her eyes. When he turns his face fully toward hers, they are inches apart. Just looking at her, his eyes go to her full luscious lips. Instinctively he reaches over placing his hand on the back of her neck pulling her into him. He moves in front of her and waits for a reaction.

She leans in, accepting his advances. Their lips meet in a sweet, slow kiss. He parts her lips with his tongue, making the kiss hot with intimacy. The kiss becomes demanding as their lips meet and part, but return immediately seeking more. Back and forth in a deep kiss, their lips become swollen with biting and sucking. One has no less aggression than the other. She is responding with abandoned desire to be touched. He has been waiting for this moment since he met her. His manhood swells as the kisses intensify.

She begins kissing the nape of his neck. As he continues kissing her neck she pulls him in, moaning with satisfaction. His hand moves to cup her breasts. He pulls the low-cut blouse down to expose the uplifting bra. He releases the top two buttons on her blouse for more access. Again, she moans with pleasure. He releases the rest of the buttons on her blouse. Looking down at her breasts, he takes in their beauty and his desire for her rages.

She unbuttons his shirt, pressing her bare breast up against his naked chest. She kisses his neck with passionate exploration. He pushes her back on the couch, moving on top of her. Fervently they devour each other with kisses while their hands explore, inspiring them to go further.

The phone rings. Not wanting to stop, they ignore it. Realizing it may be her father, Jason stops and moans in a husky voice, "You'd better get that. It could be your father checking in."

She looks at the clock on the wall for the time. It's eleven o'clock. She knew he was right, but she didn't want this to stop. She sits up to answer the phone. "Hello."

It's her father. "Hi honey, how are you feeling? You sound funny."

Flushing with the thought of what she was just doing, she says, "I'm fine, dad."

"Good, honey. Well, I'm finishing up here at the hospital. Since it's so late, would you mind if I stay at your place tonight? I don't feel like driving out to the house then back so early in the morning. My patient went through surgery better than expected, but I need to be in early to check on him in the morning."

Not that she was wishing the patient wasn't doing well, but she didn't want Jason to leave. "Dad, what time were you thinking about coming? I'm feeling tired and was about to go to bed." Looking at Jason, she smiles at that thought.

"I'm leaving now."

Not wanting to embarrass herself in front of Jason, she relents to her father coming over. "Okay dad, see you soon."

The expression of disappointment is on both of their faces. She begins putting her clothes back in order. He buttons his shirt. He picks up his phone, placing it in his back pocket.

"I guess it's time for me to leave."

"Yes, thanks to my father, the party buster."

Jason pulls her in close as they stand facing each other. "It's okay, Bridgette. I totally get it. I think this is just an excuse for your father to check in on you. I think it's bothering him that nothing showed up on your tests, so he doesn't have the scientific answers for your problem. I admit he should be relaxing over it as this point, but I think it's cute he is so protective."

"I know," she puts her arms around his neck. "I should have told him how you were taking good care of me." She smiles seductively, "You know, the extra-special exam you were just giving me."

"Ah, so that's how it is." He leans his head back and laughs. "I can tell him the physical exam went very well. I could see no problems at all." He lowers his eyes to her chest.

She giggles, "I could also tell him that I examined you to make sure I was not contagious."

Feeling himself getting hard again, he makes a decision, "I'd better get out of here before he catches us in the act."

They move to the door where they linger in each other's arms for a bit more. Kissing again, they want to go back to their earlier state of probing. He pulls away. Turning the door knob, he says, "I'll call you tomorrow." Lightly kissing her again, he leaves.

Closing the door behind him, she considers what has occurred tonight. She realizes the emotions Jason stir within her are similar to those Celeste had felt for Edward. Fear grips her. Is destiny repeating itself? Her feelings for Jason are as if she has known him all of her life. It feels so natural for him to touch her. She is unable to be coy about their attraction for each other. It is as if she is consumed by him, or under a spell. When gazing into those blue eyes, her heart swells with love. Warmth and comfort possess her at the mere thought of him.

The next day, Bridgette wakes around 8:30. She showers and fixes herself a cup of hot coffee. She hadn't waited for her father to arrive before going directly to bed last night. She looks around for him to see if he has left for the hospital yet. Of course knowing he would have morning rounds, she didn't expect to see him. She sits back on the couch, coffee in hand, thinking about what she's going to do about Celeste. The anxious feeling she has had about her has simmered since her talks with Jason. They both have come to the conclusion Celeste means her no harm. She just wants their help.

At nine-thirty, her cell phone rings. "Good morning," Jason's voice is cheerful.

"Good morning."

Jason asks, "What are you up to?"

She replies, "Just sitting here with a hot cup of coffee."

"Do you feel like some company today? I thought we'd make a day of it."

She grins entertaining the idea of a day with him. Trying to be playful she says, "Oh, your exam didn't satisfy you last night? You need more proof that I'm feeling better?"

He laughs. "Well, I'm not sure one exam is enough to come to a full diagnosis."

Sparring once more, she asks, "What areas will you examine this time?"

"Well, I need the second exam to make sure I didn't miss anything. I should review the results from yesterday, to make sure I got it right." Deciding he should stop, before his manhood becomes hard, he says, "How much time do you need to get ready?"

"Where are we going?"

"I don't have any specific plans. Just get you out of the house for some fresh air is my goal."

She replies, "That really sounds great. I have already showered, so I just need a half-hour to throw on something."

"Okay, see you in a few minutes."

He drives to her house with an excitement he hasn't experienced before. His level of interest in this woman is taking him by storm. He tries to convince himself he is just helping her, but he couldn't even wait an hour after her father called to ring her. He recalls how beautiful she was last night. He shakes his head, trying to ward off the deep emotions this woman brings to him. He has had many women coming on to him and could have had any one of them, but this one is different. All of his relationships before were so superficial. He wonders if it's because of Celeste. Is it the fact that she called him Edward? Is this some kind of destiny that he is getting caught up in? He pulls into her drive and sits there for a minute to collect his thoughts to go in. Walking up to the door, he pushes the doorbell. The door opens. He stares at this beautiful creature standing there in blue shorts, with a matching blue and white cotton tee. On her feet are bright white walking shoes. The ensemble is sporty and casual. He, too, has gone for the shorts and walking shoes. "Perfect, we think alike," he nods his head toward their outfits.

She views her outfit, and nods an agreement to the fashion statement. She walks back to the couch to get her purse, phone, and keys. They get into his 4Runner and begin the trek out of town. Windows down on a beautiful day, they ride in silence for some time.

He breaks the silence. "How did you sleep last night?"

"I slept better than I thought I would."

They spend the day talking about his job and her plans, after graduation. Neither of them have had a serious relationship. Both agree job and school have been a priority in their lives. She graduates in a couple of weeks from law school. She has been interviewing with local law firms desiring to stay in the area.

He drives her to his current job where they don hard hats, and take a tour with him pointing out specific structural designs. She could see in his face that he loves his work. He takes pride in every description he shares with her.

He looks at her and asks, "Why didn't you go into the medical field like your father?"

She smiles remembering that her mother was an attorney. "I took after my mother instead. She was a brilliant attorney, struck down in the prime of her life."

"That's too bad," he sees the sadness in her eyes. "It must have been hard on you losing her at such a young age."

"I was twelve. At first, I cried a lot missing her, but as time went on we gradually adjusted. It became a way of life. I think the hardest time for me was in my teens. I really needed the mother figure for guidance when I was going through the adolescent uncertainties. I missed the mother talks that only a mother can give. In all fairness though, my father was wonderful. Even being a doctor with long hours, he made sure I had a nanny, and was home every night right after rounds. We are very close. Of course you know that already, after all the phone calls."

He smiles, at that reminder. "There is nothing wrong with a doting father. My life was very family focused. I have a brother and a sister. We fought as kids just like all brothers and sisters do, but our love is very strong. My parents were successful entrepreneurs. My father was an architect like me. My mother was the backbone of the finances and running of the company. My brother is the CEO at Ruckensport, a research facility in Northern Virginia. My sister is a CPA with Aylor & Aylor. "

As they are getting back into the 4Runner, she says, "I do miss not having siblings growing up. You're lucky."

He looks at her and nods, "I feel lucky. I've been blessed with a wonderful family."

She asks, "Were you extra close with your dad since you went into the same profession?"

He smiles thinking of all the years he watched his father create his designs. "Yes. As a kid, I was always in his way, watching him while he worked at home. He bought me a drawing pad, so everything I saw him draw, I'd try to copy. As I grew into my teens, I would even suggest changes, and he was amazed at my insight to design. It was a forgone conclusion that architecture would be my career."

They spend the rest of the day riding the countryside admiring the beauty of the mountains. Going from overlook to overlook on the Parkway they see incredible views. He purposely avoids Celestial Manor so as not to interrupt their tranquil day. They have lunch at a small country restaurant. Pulling into her driveway at five, he jumps out to come around to help her down from the high vehicle. She falls a little toward him as she gets down. The scent of her perfume is sweet. It isn't strong, just subtle enough to arouse a man's senses.

She notices his facial expression change as she falls into him. She smiles, pulling away to reach back in to get her purse from the seat. He closes the door behind her. They walk hand-in-hand to her door.

He breaks the silence as she is unlocking the door. "Does pizza sound good for dinner?"

Keeping her eye on the lock, not turning around to show how excited she is that he wants to stay, she says, "Sure, sounds great, or I have everything to make us a chef salad."

His eyebrows shoot up. "That sounds even better."

They wash their hands and begin the prep work for the salads. Just as they are ready to sit at the table to eat, her father rings the doorbell and walks in. "Hey you two. Have the two of you been here all day?"

"No dad, we've been out all day. We rode the countryside and visited some of Jason's jobs. He does beautiful work. Sit down. I'll fix you a salad."

The three sit for a couple of hours talking. Her father talks about his patient who has made a remarkable recovery. He looks at his daughter and says, "How are you feeling, any dizziness or nausea?"

"No, it has been weeks and I feel fine. It's like nothing ever happened."

He gazes at her with a serious expression on his face. "You aren't saying that so your father won't worry are you?"

"No dad, I feel great. I don't know what happened, but I'm fine now."

Her father looks at Jason for confirmation.

"She hasn't shown any signs all day of anything being wrong."

He turns back to Bridgette, "Okay, but I need you to let me know if you have any symptoms at all."

"I will dad. I promise." She smiles at him feeling the warmth of his love. What a wonderful father she has.

Her father tells them, "Well, if you two youngsters don't mind, I'm going to head home." He looks at Bridgette and Jason, "If you need me, call me. Okay?"

"Dad, I have already promised I will call you with any symptoms." She laughs at her doting father and says, "Stop worrying. I'm fine."

He slaps the table, "Okay then, I'm out."

She walks him to the door. "Good night, Jason," her father calls out right before kissing her on the forehead as he leaves.

"Good night, Dr. Chandler."

Bridgett closes the door. Walking back to the table, she begins clearing the dishes. The two wash and dry them. They walk to the couch and begin the conversation about Celeste. They plan a visit for the following weekend to go back to Celestial Manor. Deciding to face this head on, they commit to seeing this through together. His previous hesitation to help was now gone. He was in it with her.

Feeling the relief in his commitment, she reaches over to hold his face in her hands. "Thank you, Jason. I can't tell you what this means to me. I have this urge to see this through, but I must admit I am afraid to do it alone."

Feeling her closeness, he pulls her to him. Kissing her, he lingers on her lips to taste her. Her response sends ripples of desire to his loins. Moving her hand from his face, she puts her arms around his neck to bring him closer and kisses him repeatedly. He relishes in the moment of her forwardness and sensuality. He responds with receptive reactions of greed. He wants her. He is captivated by this woman who is making him eager to explore. He moves in closer yet. Pulling her body up to his, he lingers on the kiss going deeper into the search and exploration. He kisses her down her throat, to the nape of her neck. He wastes no time pulling up and moving under her tee. He looks down at her breasts that are rising and falling. She is so aroused he can see the pulse in her neck. He stops for a moment wanting to make sure she is wanting this to continue.

"I'm more than okay. Do you think it's time to do the full exam?"

He looks at her with surprise. "You are so bad. I need to change my profession from architect to doctor." He stands holding his hand out to her and nods toward the bedroom. In agreement, she follows him without any resistance. There is enough light coming from the living room. There is no need to cut on the bedroom light.

He pulls her tee shirt over her head. She begins unbuttoning his shirt. Once separated, he assists in taking it off. They begin kissing while shedding down to their under garments. He unclips her bra and pulls the straps sensually down her shoulder, kissing her shoulders as the bra falls to the floor. Her firm upright breasts are the most beautiful breasts he has ever seen. He hardens with desire. They fall together back onto the bed, his hands exploring every part of her. Taking his time, he makes ardent love to her. Exploring, taking and giving, they both climax with fireworks taken by the frenzy of ecstasy that explodes with pulsating gratification.

Falling onto her, they both lay spent. Her chest is rising and falling against his heavy breathing. He bends his head to face hers. She looks at him with a warm, full smile. He reaches over and kisses her.

She continues to breathe heavily. "That was an intense exam."

He rolls off her laughing. "That was just the first exam. I need to repeat the exam a few more times before I am convinced that you can be released from my care."

She giggles. "What if I tell you I'm not feeling well right now?"

"Then I will need to keep a bedside vigilance until I know you're fully satisfied. I mean fully well, slip of the tongue."

They both snuggle into each other kissing and nibbling. She gets up only to get them some water and turn out the living room light. The moonlight shining through the window lights the room as she returns. He watches the beautiful figure of the woman returning to bed. His heart strings tug. He is leaning on the headboard accepting the glass of water. He drinks it down quenching his thirst. She places the empty glasses on the night stand then crawls back into bed beside him. They cuddle in silence. No one mentions that he should leave, but takes it for granted he is where he should be. Right before he falls asleep, he whispers, "I feel like Edward."

She hears his words and says nothing. She ponders those words and what he could have meant by them. The one thing she knows is that Edward loved Celeste. Maybe he was going there. She falls asleep with a smile on her face.

CHAPTER 19

FACING HER FEARS

Bridgette awakes the next morning rejuvenated. Her night of love making with Jason puts a new pep in her step. She has not been with anyone for a very long time. She has never been with anyone that made her feel like Jason did last night. They couldn't keep their hands off each other. Sleeping occurred sporadically throughout the night. Each time they made love, it was better than the last. As she looks over at the sleeping, beautiful man in her bed, she tries to find nagging doubts. They should be creeping in when two people make love for the first time. She could not muster the doubts.

Jason opens his eyes to find Bridgette bringing in two cups of hot coffee. He sits up and props his pillows to lean on. Keeping the sheet over his naked body, he takes the cup gratefully and sips slowly. "Thank you. With the little sleep I got last night, I need this for energy. It's not decaffeinated, is it?"

"No, it's the hard stuff," she smiles over the top of her cup.

She crawls back into bed beside him, leaving on the silk robe she had donned.

Sitting the cup on the night stand after a few sips he reaches over to her. "Come here woman." He kisses her passionately. He lays his hand over her breast on top of the silk material.

She moans, "Stop it," pushing his hands away. "Do you ever quit?" She beams a she-devil smile, while pushing him back.

"Do you want me to stop?"

She gives him a smile that leaves him guessing.

Jason pulls her in close to him.

They lay there snuggling in silence for a moment. She is almost to the point of falling off to sleep when he says, "Are you okay with all of this?"

"It's a little late to ask that question isn't it? Does it feel like it's okay with me?"

He laughs. "Yes, I guess it is a little late, but I want this to be acceptable to you." Laughing again, he says, "Oh yes, it did feel as if you were okay with it. If not, you're a great actress."

She looks up into those blue eyes and sees the tenderness. "I'm more than okay with it."

"Good. I'm pleased that you are."

With that agreement, they both fall asleep. Waking hours later, she leans up to view the clock. It's eleven o'clock, almost lunch time. She nudges Jason, "Do you know it's eleven?"

Rising to look at the clock, he lies back, "You got somewhere to be?"

Realizing his contentment to be there, she relaxes in his arms to enjoy the warmth of his body. "No, I don't have any plans today."

Lying there relaxed together, they decide to go to Celestial Manor. She picks up her phone from the night stand to find out if it's even open on Sundays. "It's open from one to five," she waits to see if he is interested in going today.

"If you want to go, I'm game. Are you sure you're okay?"

She kisses him then jumps up. "Yes, I'm sure. You get a shower in there," motioning toward the master bath, "while I make breakfast."

He agrees. Getting up, he heads to the bathroom.

She points, "There are extra razors, and a new toothbrush in the medicine cabinet." She smiles to herself realizing that buying the two-pack of razors and tooth brushes that she thought was a waste, has now turned into an advantage.

"Okay, thanks."

She puts the biscuits in the oven, starting the bacon in the skillet on low. She runs quickly to the main bathroom, and jumps in the shower while they cook. She is so quick, she beats him out of the shower. He walks out with his shorts on and says, "I'll be back in a minute." He goes out to the back of the 4Runner and returns with an overnight bag. Returning to the bedroom, he is back in moments in a new set of shorts and shirt.

She says laughing, "Wow, was that planned?"

He searches for seriousness and sees the smiling face, then laughs out a no. "I always keep several changes of clothes in my vehicle. I have business casual, and something for relaxing. I go to some construction sites that are filthy, and can come out of there pretty dirty. I never want to be in a position not to be able to change if a meeting is to follow. I also keep several business suites at work if needed. I'm a planner as you can now see."

"That's actually a really good idea," she acknowledges the cleverness.

Looking at her wet hair, "Wow, you've already showered too?"

"Yes, I used the main bath. I ran in and took a quick one." She pours the scrambled eggs onto their plates with a biscuit and 2 slices of bacon. She places the hot skillet back on the stove.

He watches her, "That really smells good. I'm famished."

She asks, "Worked up an appetite did you?"

He looks at her. With no makeup on, she is still gorgeous. He smiles and walks around the table to pull her back into him. Nuzzling her neck he mumbles, "Yes, and then some."

She turns around giving him a passionate kiss. "I'm really enjoying this."

"Me, too."

They sit talking, discussing their anticipation of the visit. They wrap up breakfast and leave. Both wonder if Celeste will show herself.

Pulling into the long drive, she gets very nervous.

Hearing her taking a deep breath, he tries to comfort her. "I'm here for you."

"I'm just anxious."

"Say the word and we'll leave."

She slowly responds, "No, I need to do this. I want to help her."

"Jason watches the ominous building as they approach. He says, "I do, too."

They walk in and pay for the individual tour instead of the group tour. They head up to the room where they both have seen her. Entering the room, Jason closes the door behind them.

Bridgette sees him closing the door and asks, "What are you doing, Jason?"

"Bridgette, we don't want others to see what is going on if she shows herself. We don't want any interruptions."

She takes a nervous breath and agrees.

Once the door closes, they walk around the room looking at items that belonged to Edward and Celeste. Bridgette recognizes a lot of the items in the room. Every item she sees is something she remembers, only reassuring her that what Celeste had shown her during her coma was real.

She picks up the hairbrush on the dressing table. She glances in the mirror and sees Celeste standing right behind her. Dropping the brush she quickly turns around to face Celeste.

Jason hears the brush drop, and briskly turns toward Bridgette. In front of Bridgette stands Celeste. He's amazed at the resemblance of the two women. The only difference is that Celeste has the tight curls, while Bridgette's hair has loose curls. He rushes to Bridgette's side.

Celeste is so happy to see Bridgette. For the first time since they have met her, she has a smile on her face. She says, "Thank you for coming, Bridgette." She looks toward Jason, "Edward." She moves toward Jason and says, "My darling."

Too afraid to correct her, Jason replies, "It's okay, Celeste. Go to the light. I'm waiting for you there."

Celeste feels confused. "No, Edward. I went to the light, but you were not there."

Bridgette sees the pain in Celeste's face and says, "It's okay, Celeste. We are here to help you find your way. She lays her hand on Jason's shoulder and says, "This is not Edward, this is Jason. We have come to help you find your way to Edward."

Celeste feels confused. Looking away from Jason to Bridgette, she says, "No, this is Edward. I can see his blue eyes. No one has the blue eyes like Edward. You can swim in them." She turns back to Jason for confirmation.

Bridgette sympathizes with her, "I know they are beautiful. Celeste, I want to thank you for sharing your life with me."

She looks at Bridgette and acknowledges. "Yes, I had to make you see the love we shared. Edward is part of me. I cannot go on without him. It has been so long since I have seen him." A tear runs down her face as she continues. "I have roamed these halls for a very long time waiting for him to return to me."

Bridgette feels bad for her. "I know you have, Celeste. We are going to try to find a way to reunite the two of you."

Celeste looks back at Jason. "If you are not Edward, then why do you look so much like him?"

Jason replies, "I'm not sure, Celeste. I don't know if fate has brought me to you and Bridgette or what, but I want to help you." Jason looks over at Bridgette, who is now emotionally invested. A tear drops out of the corner of her eye.

Bridgette is overwhelmed with sorrow for Celeste. Having felt her pain and love for Edward while in the coma, she is desperate to make things right.

Celeste watches the two of them. Moving from one face to the other, she recognizes the familiarity. "The two of you look like Edward and me." Landing on Bridgette's face she says, "I feel like I am looking in the mirror when I see you."

Bridgette's heart explodes. "You are my great, great grandmother."

Celeste appears astonished. "Yes, it is all so clear now. I can see that you are a part of me." She realizes the depth of what has transpired here. Celeste asks Jason to leave the room for a minute.

He gives a worried look toward Bridgette, "Celeste, I can't do that. I can't let you hurt Bridgette again."

Celeste is shocked at his words. "I would never hurt my great, great grand-daughter. I just need to speak to her privately."

Jason seeks an answer from Bridgette to his leaving the room. She nods that it is okay, so he leaves.

Once out of the room, Celeste shares her thoughts. "Bridgette, the only thing that will bring Edward back is if love is found in this home again. If Jason is not Edward, then Jason's love for you has to bring Edward back to me."

Recognizing Celeste's train of thought, she tells Celeste that she and Jason only just met a few months ago. They are not in love.

Disappointment shadows Celeste's face. Then he must be the one to bring Edward to me. Could he be Edward? Are you bringing him back to me?"

Thinking about their night together, guilt fills Bridgette. What if Jason is Edward re-incarnated? That would be horrible. Her great, great grandfather just made love to her all night. Not willing to accept that conclusion she responds, "No, I don't think Jason is Edward."

"Then he must love you to bring love back to this house. Edward will return when love is present."

Bridgette feels a concern for the plan. She just met Jason. Today is nothing like the early 1900s. Edward and Celeste did not consummate their love until marriage. She has known Jason for only a few months and has already made love to him. That does not constitute him loving her like Edward loved Celeste. Things are different now.

"When the two of you return love to this house, Edward will come." As Jason opens the door to re-enter she whispers, "He must not know. He must truly love you for this to happen."

Embarrassed as Jason walks toward her, Bridgette feels hopelessly out of control with the request that Celeste has put forth.

Jason, noticing Bridgette's discomfort, gives her a concerned look.

Celeste disappears.

She takes Jason's hand and pulls him from the room. They walk in silence out to the 4Runner. Jason breaks the silence once inside the vehicle. "What did she say to you?"

Without telling him he has a major role in Celeste's plan, she says, "I think she wants me to move into the house to bring love back."

He asks, "Into that Mausoleum?"

Bridgette replies in frustration with his words, "That is not how she sees this place, Jason. This is where she lived with Edward in happiness."

"I understand that, but in today's time, this place is enormous compared to normal living. The upkeep alone would be astronomical."

Still feeling frustrated at his lack of understanding, Bridgette shoots back. "Jason, it's not worth discussing, I couldn't afford this place anyway."

Jason asks, "Would you do it if you could afford it?"

Without looking toward Jason, she stares out the window "Yes, I would do this to help her if that is what it took."

Jason shakes his head in disbelief. "Wow, she has gotten to you hasn't she?"

A tear falls down Bridgette's face. Keeping her face away from Jason, so he won't see her tears, she says, "She is my great, great grandmother, Jason. My heart bleeds for her. She's family."

He can hear the quiver in her voice, so he backs off. "I guess I get it."

Frustrated with his lack of empathy, she says, "It doesn't matter if you get it. I will find a way to help her." As they ride back to her place, she is mad at herself for getting frustrated with Jason. This was no way to accomplish Celeste's request that Jason would need to love her in order to reach Edward. She must find a way on her own to get Edward to return. Dependence on another for Celeste's happiness cannot be contingent on Jason. She doesn't even know her own feelings for him. Could she love this man herself?

They reached her apartment at four. He decides to go in for a minute, but senses Bridgette wants him to leave. He makes an effort to show comfort. She places her keys and purse on the entry table. He walks up behind her and snuggles into her, wrapping his arms around her waist. She turns toward him and brings him in close wrapping her arms around his neck so she doesn't have to look him in the eyes. They stand in silence in their embrace for a while.

He pulls back searching her face. "What did she say to upset you so much?"

"I don't want to talk about this anymore."

He looks concerned. "Okay," squeezing her tightly. "I'll get out of here and let you process this. Will you give me a call when you're ready to see me again?"

"Sure." She kisses him softly and begins backing away from him.

"Oh, no you don't. I will not leave with a lackluster kiss like that."

She smiles at this, and the comfort of last night resurfaces her emotions. She kisses him deeply. They begin heavy petting and soon he is backing her into the bedroom. She puts herself whole heartedly into the moment and greedily takes him. All the frustrations of the day disappear as love fills the room.

Lying there afterward, she is back to the warm feelings she had of him last night. She apologizes to him for her earlier frustrations. Bridgette tells him she is frustrated on how to help Celeste. He says he understands and kisses her repeatedly. "Celeste is lucky to have you in her corner."

He leaves after cuddling for hours. Holding her in his arms feels right to him. He hates to leave her, and postpones it until he no longer can. Bridgette takes time after he leaves to review the day before she sleeps. After a hot shower, she crawls into bed. Her mind is so busy thinking about what has occurred this weekend with Jason and Celeste. She does really like Jason, and has enjoyed his company, particularly his lovemaking. She smiles to herself remembering the hot sex they just had. I guess if I had to love someone, he would be a great choice. She thinks it too soon to love him. Heck, they have only been together for a few months, but this weekend changed everything between them. They moved to the next step in their relationship. Having sex always complicates emotions. How will she get him to love her for Celeste? She decides as she is dropping off to sleep it can't be forced. If they are to love, it has to happen in their time. As that thought passes, she falls off to sleep.

CHAPTER 20

WHAT IS THE NEW NORMAL?

Bridgette gets to class early Monday with new enthusiasm to finish her last semester. She needs the distraction from the past months. Having gone through Celeste and Edward's life, it seems longer. She has final exams in a couple of weeks prior to graduation, so she needs to focus. Diving into her studies, she pulls her thoughts away from Jason.

The next couple of weeks fly by. Studying non-stop for exams creates the diversion she needs. Her dad checks in on her regularly, but she assures him each time she is fine. Jason calls wanting to set up plans to get together. She assures him that as soon as she gets through the next few weeks, they can make plans. She is just too pressed right now to take the time out from studies. Having been through those days in college himself, he totally understands, sort of.

On the last week, the night before one of her exams, the doorbell rings. She leaves her office with books scattered on the desk. Assuming it's her dad, she opens the door, but finds Jason.

For weeks, Jason can think of nothing other than Bridgette. He is consumed with her. He has never had a woman deny his company before, especially after their passionate weekend. He understands her commitment, but feels she could at least take time out for lunch or something. Stopping by with the pizza feels like a great idea. He doesn't think he could go another day without seeing her.

She looks at him and smiles. "What are you doing here?"

He pushes his way past her, holding the pizza under her nose as he passes. "I know you need to stop long enough to eat, so thus, the pizza."

Smelling the aroma of the pizza made her realize how hungry she was. To think of it, she hadn't stopped to eat lunch today either.

Jason sets the pizza on the table then reaches in the cabinet for plates. She walks over to the refrigerator and pulls out some chilled wine. I guess it won't hurt to stop for a bit she decides to herself. Looking at that handsome face warms her. She finds she is glad he stopped by even though her recent protests for company had pushed him away. She was glad she had the break from him so she could control not getting swept up in their last weekend. Having the time away from him made her think more clearly. Seeing him spreads warmth over her. His smile can shake her world.

They sit at the table and talk for a half hour. Jason looks at his watch and says, "How much studying do you have to do tonight?"

"I think I'm almost done. I just need to review the question and answers at the end of each chapter. After that, I think I'm ready. The exam tomorrow is the tough one. There was no opting out of this one. The others are a piece of cake. In fact, tomorrow I will find out if I have aced out of taking the other exams. It will depend on my final grades for the classes."

Jason says, "Wow, beautiful and smart!" His dimples deepen as his grin widens.

She smiles.

"How about me quizzing you?"

"Jason, you don't have to do that. I'm sure you have other things you need to do. It's a weeknight. You need to work tomorrow."

He smiles at her. "Yes I do, but a little less sleep won't kill me."

She goes to her office and grabs the textbook. She shows him the questions at the end of each chapter that she needs to review. He begins the questions. He is amazed at how smart she is. Without hesitation, she answers each question thoroughly. There was only one question that tripped her up, but that was because the question was not clearly stated. She thought they were asking one thing, but in fact it was the opposite. Once that was clear, she aced it.

Glancing at the clock and seeing its ten o'clock, she says, "Well, we have done all we can do."

As they rise from the table, she thanks him for his help. She walks him to the door. Blocking her from opening the door, he pulls her into his arms. She willingly falls in as he kisses her gently. He says, "Good-luck tomorrow."

"Thanks Jason. I really appreciate you stopping by and helping with my studies. I would never have agreed to you coming over otherwise. My focus needed to be on this huge test."

"I knew that. I took my chances anyway. Darn glad I did." He kisses her one more time before turning the door knob to leave.

Just as he is about to close the door, Bridgette pulls it back open and kisses him one more time. Somewhat surprised, he gladly responds. Those dimples deepen. She shoves him away before she does something she will regret. She needs a good night's sleep so she can focus tomorrow.

The next morning she gets the results of opting out of some exams. This exam was not available for opting out. Finding out she does not have to take any more exams relieves some tension for her. She sits to get this one over with. She is well prepared. She walks away finishing the test in just a half hour. All of her preparations paid off. She walks out of class realizing she just graduated. She has no more classes. Even though there is one more week of exams with the school, she has met the requirements to graduate. She drives home. Relief overtaking her, she goes to her bedroom and falls into bed. She has stayed up late many nights this week preparing for the tests that are now finally over. The exhaustion hits her. She falls into a deep sleep. When she wakes up, it's dark in her apartment. Reaching over to turn on the light, she sits up feeling a little groggy. She showers and puts on some comfy PJ's. She turns on the TV to a movie that she immerses herself in. Feeling the weight off of her for school, she now thinks about getting a job. She shuts off the TV at midnight and goes back to bed.

The next morning she is wakened by the phone. She looks at the clock and sees it's nine o'clock. Surprised she has slept so late after having slept half the day away yesterday was a surprise. "Hello."

The voice says, "Ms. Bridgette Chandler please."

"Speaking," she says in response.

"Bridgette, this is Victor, from Celestial Manor."

"Hello, Victor. How are you?"

"I've had better days," he assures her.

"I'm sorry Victor, what's wrong?"

"It's Mr. Barkley. I'm afraid he passed away last week."

The shock of this news shakes her to the core. "Oh my," she says in a stunned voice. "How did it happen?" Surely convinced there was some kind of accident.

Victor continues, "He had been having some health issues in recent months. When he went to the doctor, they found he had stage four cancer. It had spread to the lymph nodes and his liver. His body just shut down."

"I'm so sorry Victor. I know the two of you were close. This must be so difficult for you."

Victor says, "It's very hard on me. We were business partners, but he was my best friend as well."

She understands, "Yes, I could feel there was mutual respect when you two were together."

"Bridgette, the reason I'm calling is because there will be a reading of his will tomorrow at ten o'clock. You've been listed in his will, so your presence is requested."

Stunned silent, she hesitates with her response. "What? There must be some mistake Victor. I barely knew him."

Victor tells her, "I think it will all become clear tomorrow. Can you make it? I've assured the attorney that you will be there."

"Sure Victor, I would be honored to pay my respects."

After hanging up the phone, she doesn't know what to think. She had been so busy these past few weeks. She must have missed the death announcement in the paper. She barely knew this man. She picks up the phone to call Jason. When he answers, she tells him about the phone call.

Like Bridgette, he is just as surprised. "Well let's do lunch tomorrow after you go there. I will die of curiosity until I hear from you."

"Sounds good, I'll see you then." They make plans to meet at the same restaurant they had met before.

The next morning she adorns a dark navy blue dress. While putting on her makeup, she contemplates the meeting, imagining all kinds of things. Nothing would be answered until she gets there. She takes a final look in the mirror, grabs her phone, purse, and keys to leave.

She knows the law firm Victor had mentioned. She found it without trouble. She had in fact considered applying there for a job. Walking into the suite on the 7th floor, she spots Victor right away. He walks over to her, "They just came to tell me when you arrive we can come in."

She is confused, "Okay sure, let's go in."

The office is elegant and large. The huge desk made of Rosewood is sparsely decorated. The attorney stands up at the entrance and points to the long conference table on the other side of the room. She nods and walks with Victor to the table. Once everyone is seated (and by everyone, it was just the attorney, Victor, and Bridgette), the attorney begins the reading of the will.

Victor is named sole heir of a life insurance policy that is eight million dollars. The shock on Victor's face told her that this was unexpected news. He names off properties that Victor will now be owner of. Every asset Mr. Barkley has will be turned over into Victor's name. He may do as he pleases with them. He can sell or keep them for property income. He has Mr. Barkley's blessing on whatever decision he makes.

Next he turns to Bridgette. "Ms. Chandler, Mr. Barkley has left the Celestial Manor estate to you. Realizing this will be a monstrosity for upkeep, he has also left a dowry of ten million dollars to assist with that. Mr. Barkley had begun selling off some of his assets. Other than what he has left for Victor, this ten million is from selling those assets. Mr. Barkley has no descendants, so his wish was that you have your great, great grand-mother's estate."

In total for Victor and Bridgette, the man was worth forty million dollars. The astonishment of this revelation has put her into a state of numbness. She sits, not knowing how to respond. She hadn't realized this man was so rich.

The attorney, seeing her surprised expression, nods in understanding. He moves two sets of documents to both Victor and Bridgette. "I will need both of you to sign these documents. I will get the legal work completed, and all assets moved over to the two of you. After signing the documents, both leave in silence. Once outside, Victor turns to her and says, "Bridgette, I know this is a little over the top for you, but I need to tell you something. Mr. Barkley was so happy to have someone to leave his money to. He had no relatives to give anything to. It was his greatest pleasure to return Celestial Manor to your family."

"Thank you for sharing this Victor. I feel so bad. I barely knew him." Reviewing the events in her mind, she says, "I'm in shock."

"I know you are Bridgette, but I think this is what Celeste would want. Maybe she can find peace in knowing you now own it. It's back in the family as it should be. He has left you enough money to do whatever you want with it."

She thanks Victor, and they part ways. Driving to meet Jason, she wonders what Jason and her father will think of this. Pulling into the parking lot, she spots his Mercedes immediately. She is about ten minutes late. She pulls in beside him.

She gets out as he opens the door for her. She pecks him on the lips. He tells her they need to hurry in. They are late for their reservation. Once seated in a private section of the restaurant, Jason says, "I thought a little privacy would be needed to discuss what happened this morning during the reading of the will. Why were you requested to be there?"

After telling him everything that occurred, he was speechless. "OMG," he is shocked.

"I know. Your expression is exactly what I had when he told me."

Jason looks at her then questions her. "What are you going to do with that place?"

"I don't know Jason. I'm still in shock. I need to discuss this with my father. He may have some advice."

"I would love to be a fly on the wall to see the expression on his shocked face."

She sighs, "I left him a message that I'd like to have dinner with him tonight."

Jason looks at her while shaking his head. "Your father is going to freak out. You are an overnight millionaire. How do you think he will take it?"

"My father comes from wealth, so the money won't shock him. Well, I guess the venue that it came from might shock him, but Celestial Manor is the news that may be hard for him to swallow."

Jason says, "Yeah, I can see that." He is so blown away he can't change the subject. "What are your plans for it?"

"Jason, I have no earthly idea. I do know I need to tell Celeste. I wonder if this will give her some peace."

Jason replies, "You know, I never thought about that. To have her home back in the family may calm her enough to let go."

Bridgette stirs the spoon around in her tea. "I hope so, Jason. I want to help her."

Jason says, "So how did the exam go yesterday?"

She says, "I was amazed at how easy it was. I really appreciate your help. The questions we reviewed were the very questions on the test, so I think I aced it."

"Good for you. How many more do you have now?"

"I'm done."

"Great, so can I take you out to celebrate?"

She says, "I want to meet with dad tonight. How about Friday night? Will that work for you?"

He motions for the waiter, "Sure, that works." Placing a tip on the table and signing the check, they walk out. He looks at her and all he sees is a beautiful woman. "I've never met a woman like you. There are so many twists and turns in your life that I can't keep up." He bends and lightly kisses her at the car. He tells her he will see her on Friday, then rushes off back to work.

That night she tells her father what happened at the reading of the will. He is shocked to say the least. "What are you going to do with that place, honey?"

"Well, dad, I have a thought in mind. I wanted to hear what you think about the idea."

"Okay, I'm listening."

She shares her newfound plans. "It's so large. I was thinking about turning it into a lodge for executive retreats." There are so many rooms, I think it would work. It has the big dining hall where we could have a small restaurant. What do you think?"

He thinks about the idea for a minute and says, "That would be a huge undertaking. What kind of condition is it in?"

"Well, it does need some upgrades. Remember, they are still functioning on the property's power house for electricity. It would need total wiring and new mechanical systems for heat and air conditioning. We would need to install bathrooms in every suite."

He smiles, "You have given this some thought, I see."

"Dad, I think it would be so much fun to make that place beautiful again. I would make it an upscale lodge with special amenities."

He says, "That will cost you a ton of money."

"Dad, I told you he left me money for upkeep, but I didn't tell you how much."

He smiles and says, "I'm sure it's not enough for this undertaking."

She smiles before she emphasizes the amount, "Ten million dollars."

Astonished he says, "What? Are you kidding me? Why would this stranger leave you ten million dollars?"

"Dad, he had no relatives and had planned to give it all to charity until he saw Celeste and our resemblances. He felt compelled to do this for her, not me."

"What did he know about Celeste? She wasn't the owner he purchased it."

"I think it was because I look so much like her, he became interested in her history." She was not about to tell her father about all of them seeing her ghost. He would not be on board with her keeping the place if he knew all about that.

"Well, I guess I can see that." He looks at his daughter and says, "Are you up to the challenge this renovation will bring?"

She replies, "Who knows, dad. I plan to ask Jason for some advice on it. In fact, I thought about contracting him to handle it all."

Her dad nods his head in agreement. "Does he have the time available for it? He is a well sought-after architect from what I hear."

"I don't know, but I plan to ask."

Her dad takes a sip of his wine and asks, "So what's the deal with you two? Are you dating, serious or what?"

"We like each other. It's really too soon to know if anything will come of it. I like him."

"By what I have been seeing, it seems he *likes* you too." He says those words emphasizing the like as if like is an understatement.

She laughs. "Dad, if a man looks at me, you think he wants to get married. Chill out, I'm in no hurry to go beyond what I have now. We are having fun together."

"Back to your project, what does this mean for you getting a job in a law firm? Will you be holding off on that?"

"I don't know. I think I'll play it by ear. I have received a few offers from some small firms, but not what I am hoping for. Now, I guess I will need to understand how involved I will need to be for the remodeling. If I hire it out, I may be able to do both. We'll see."

Drinking the last sip in his glass, he says, "Well, honey, I have an early morning tomorrow so I'd better get home. Are you okay now? Are you having any symptoms or dizziness?"

As she walks him to the door she responds, "No, I feel fine. Whatever it was is over now."

He gives her a bear hug and says, "I hope so, honey. Good night. Lock the door behind me."

She laughs. "Dad, will you ever stop treating me like a little girl?"

He smiles, "Not on your life!"

"Good night, dad."

"Good night, honey."

CHAPTER 21

ALL IN A DAYS WORK

On Friday night, Jason picks Bridgette up at seven. He takes her to the theatre then to dinner. It's a great distraction from everyday life. As they pull up to her place, she tells him what a wonderful time she has had. "Do you have time enough to come in? There's something I want to talk over with you."

He turns the car off, "Sure, what's on your mind?"

"Come on in. I'll get us a glass of wine."

They go inside. As she gets the glasses from the cabinet she says, "Jason, you are in the business of building and design, so I need some advice on what to do with Celestial Manor."

He says okay with growing interest.

"I'm thinking about renovating, and turning it into a lodge. What do you think about that? Is it structurally sound for the foot traffic involved?"

He takes a sip of wine as he thinks, "Well, I did see some issues with it when I took the tour. I would need to investigate it thoroughly. I wasn't inspecting for structural defects at the time."

"Oh, I know there is a lot of work needed, but my main concern is could it be turned into a lodge for business retreats?"

"Why don't we do a tour, to specifically look at the structure? Want to ride up there tomorrow? Are they still giving tours?"

She reaches in a glass bowl on the counter. Smiling, she pulls out a set of keys. The key ring was huge with loads of keys. "Tours have stopped, I have the keys now."

He laughs, "The keys are labeled. I hope."

"I know this big one goes to the front door."

Settling on the trip for tomorrow, they sit on the couch. "I have another question for you."

"Shoot."

She asks, "Would you have time to oversee the remodel? Does your firm do that type of work?"

"Well, I have never personally handled a remodel, but I have a team that does."

She asks, "How much do you think it will cost to renovate it?"

Rubbing his chin, he says, "I would say at least three million, granted that there are no structural damages that would need repair. It could cost as much as five million if there are issues. Let's go up tomorrow to take a look with the eye of an architect before we speculate."

"That sounds great, and thanks for letting me drag you into this adventure."

He pulls her chin up to him, "You will owe me."

Decision made, she leans in to kiss him. She snuggles and says seductively, "I have missed you these past few weeks. You have some making up to do."

His dimples deepen. "Wait just a minute. I was the one that kept calling to see you, but you didn't have the time. You, my lady, have some making up to do to me."

They move to the bedroom as they are kissing. He pushes her in front of the bed. One by one he assists her in shedding her clothes down to her lingerie. They lay back on the bed. Climbing on top of her, she unbuttons his shirt and belt of his trousers. He removes his clothes down to his jocks. The night is full of passion, making up for time lost the last few weeks. They sleep in each other's arms satiated and assuaged.

The time away from Bridgette makes him crazy. His thoughts are only of her. Touching her tonight was more than lust, it was full of warmth. Touching her tan skin with his fingers, he is overtaken with emotions that he is unable to push away. In only a short time, she has become his everything. He admits to himself he is in love for the very first time in his life.

Bridgette looks into his beautiful blue eyes. Removing the physical attraction she has for him, she loves his smile. She loves the way his eyes smile when he smiles. His humor always keeps them on the light side of things. He grounds her. The fact that he is taking on the issue with Celeste only makes her fall for him more each day. She is falling in love with this man, with each and every day she spends with him.

The next morning they lie in bed lazily, first discussing Celestial Manor then moving on to a critical topic.

Bridgette starts the conversation with, "Jason, are you sleeping with anyone else?"

Shocked at the question, he says, "No, are you?"

"No, I'm not. I think we should discuss what is going on between us."

He says, "I couldn't agree more. What's going on?"

She turns quickly to give him a serious face.

He lays his hand on her stomach in a reassuring way. "What I mean is, I know what I hope is going on, but I'm not sure. You've been pretty closed lipped about your feelings."

"So have you."

"I think we both have been pretty guarded with words," he says gazing into her gray blue eyes.

She rubs his arm up and down, moving the hair on his arm into place. "I haven't known what to think. We haven't known each other that long. It's important now though that we clear up what is going on between us. You are a very handsome man, Jason. I know women flock to you. I will not sleep with a man that is sleeping around."

"I feel the same way. Let me ask you the same question. Are you seeing anyone else?"

She looks into his blue eyes and sees love there. "No, I'm seeing no one else."

Relief shows on his face. "Do we want to label this?"

"What do you mean?"

"Well are we casually dating, but not sleeping with anyone else? Are we friends with benefits?" He gives her a smirk as he says that. "Are we in a committed relationship? What is it?"

She's afraid to show her hand first so she evades, "What do you think it is?"

Sounding a little frustrated he questions her. "Come on, Bridgette. Are you in this with me or are you not?"

She gets a huge grin on her face, "That is exactly what I wanted to hear." She reaches up and pulls his head down to hers. She kisses him deeply. "Does this answer your question?"

He responds, "No, that says you want something." He motions to his manhood.

She laughs, "That, too."

"What am I going to do with you?"

She replies, "Anything you want."

"Okay, I can do that, but first, are we in a committed relationship?"

"I am if you are. Can we take this one day at a time for a while? Let's discover what we have as we go."

He laughs, "You are the first woman to make me crazy! I'm willing to see where this goes. Deal?"

She laughs at his playfulness, "Deal."

They ride up to Celestial Manor at one o'clock. They tour the grounds first, and then go inside to take measurements and notes. He talks through each issue, while she takes notes. She is now seeing the professional side of Jason. He is so manly, controlling, and factual. He knows his craft. Getting to know this side of him is taking her to another level of respect. After finishing the tour, he says, "Sure, I think the lodge will work. You need to decide what you want regarding each space. Looking at the kitchen area and the large dining hall, it would be a nice quaint restaurant or food space for guests. Kind of like a bed and breakfast. You could get about 15 suites on the two upper floors. The inside needs to be brought up to date. It will need new plumbing throughout the whole house, electrical, and I would take down the plaster and do drywall. I saw some water leakage near the towers. That will need to be fixed."

She reads down the list of notes. She asks, "Okay, so you think it's achievable?"

He observes the beautiful manor and says, "I think it would be gorgeous. You could make this into an upscale business retreat."

She hugs him. "I'm getting excited with the prospects."

He hugs her back. "You do know this will be a huge undertaking. What are your plans for a job? Will the remodel be your job?" He looks around and says, "It will be a job." He turns back toward her to see if she is ready to accept it.

"I want to move on it, what do you think? How quickly can we get started?"

Standing in each other's arms he asks, "Aren't you forgetting something?"

She searches his face for the answer.

"Celeste. Don't you think you need to tell her?"

She stops dead still. "You're right. We need to tell her."

They go to Celeste's room hoping she will appear. When she doesn't show herself, Bridgette tells her about Celestial Manor now belonging to her. Slowly, Celeste appears. Tears are streaming down her face. "My home belongs to my great, great granddaughter. That is wonderful. Will you and Jason be getting married and moving here?"

"No. Celeste, we want to open this home for others to stay and enjoy the beauty of it. Is that okay with you? Jason won't be moving in, but when the construction has been completed and repairs made, I will be moving in."

Celeste looks at Jason, then back to Bridgette. "Love must live here. It is the only way Edward will return to me."

Bridgette moves toward her, "Celeste, I love you already. Love is here. I will do everything I can to get Edward back to you. I promise."

"Edward will come?"

Jason says, "We will do everything we can to make that happen, I promise. We don't want to upset you with the construction we will be doing on Celestial Manor. Will you be okay?"

Celeste replies, "It will be good to have people around me again. It has been quiet too long."

Bridgette pleads, "Celeste, please only show yourself to Jason and myself. We don't want to alarm anyone. Can you do that?"

Celeste says, "I only show myself when love is present."

Bridgette looks at Jason and smiles.

Celeste looks at the two of them and says, "The two of you will bring my Edward back to me. I know it."

Bridgette sighs, "I wish I could hug you."

Tears fall down Celeste's face, "You are in my heart. I love you." She disappears.

Jason and Bridgette leave Celestial Manor. They talk of the love that Edward and Celeste share. It takes her three hours to tell Jason the complete experience she had when Celeste had shown it to her during the coma. She goes into greater details than when she had discussed it the first time. He is amazed. It makes him feel the pain she must be in. He says, "We have to help her."

Bridgette's only response is, "Yes, we do." She cannot tell him that Celeste thinks *their* love will bring Edward back.

CHAPTER 22

BREATHTAKING

Jason gets started on Celestial Manor right away. They meet regularly to go over the designs, formal and informal. They meet at Jason's office or with his construction workers on site when they are not glued to her dining room table reviewing the sketches.

After months of design and redesign, they have finally come up with an exceptional plan. The construction work begins by tearing out the plaster walls, and replacing all plumbing and electrical. Bathrooms are added to each suite. Outside construction starts immediately. Repairing stone, cracks, and some defects outside renders a month of unstable areas around the premises. Special care is needed when inspecting the work. Each day breathes new life into the neglected manor. Three months pass before Bridgette can actually see it coming to life.

During this time, Bridgette has checked in with Celeste to make sure she hasn't been disturbed by the construction activities. Celeste is comforted by the changes. She is glad her house is no longer falling into disrepair. She and Bridgette are close, taking walks together. With coaching to go beyond the walls of Celestial Manor, they even visit Edward's grave. Celeste finds it disturbing to see her own name on a headstone over a grave. Bridgette assures her that she is not there. The only thing in that grave is an earthly body that is no longer useful to her. She assures her that Edward is not there either. She will see him again, she is sure of it.

Jason makes extra visits to Celestial Manor to make sure everything is on target with the design plan. Occasionally he has to tweak a few things. With Bridgette's consent, the alterations go smoothly. He doesn't see Celeste at all when he roams the property for inspections. He stands staring at the place. The improvements are stunning. Bridgette's designs are making the place a work of art. He is proud to be a part of it.

Along with the property, another house had been built. Bridgette decides that instead of living at Celestial Manor, she will move into that house. Jason hires a separate crew to begin the remodel. She and Jason decide together what is needed and the style she wishes to achieve. She delicately asks him to provide his input on the remodeling. She wants it to reflect both masculine and feminine.

He looks at her when she asks and pauses.

She says, "Well, I do hope to get married one day."

He smiles and from then on, gives her input on what he would like to see if it were his.

Their relationship is maintaining a constant pattern of growth. He stays at her place a lot, which she is learning to enjoy. On nights he doesn't stay over, she finds she misses him. Their business and personal relationship mingles well with the constant demands of work involved with adding the house renovations onto the manor restoration project. To keep the historical feel of the property, she selects the neo-classical architecture design. Several bedrooms are on the main floor, with guest suites on the top floor. With Jason's expertise on design, she couldn't be happier with the results.

By the end of summer, the house is ready to move into. Weeks before he releases the house to her, they are lying in bed after an exceptional hour of love-making. Jason's heart has been committed to her from the start, but no discussions have occurred about their relationship since the morning they talked about a commitment. He is holding her in his arms when he says, "Bridgette, I don't know if you are ready to hear this, but I love you." He couldn't see her face when he says it because she was cuddled under his arm, her face toward his chest. He received silence from her.

Bridgette hears the words and wants to cry. She has been in love with Jason for months now. This was what she had hoped for, not only for Celeste, but her heart has opened wide for him. She closes her eyes.

His finger goes under her chin to lift her face up toward him. "No comment?"

Emotions exploding and a lump in her throat, she says, "Jason, I love you, too." She looks into those bright blue eyes and sees love. When he smiles at her declaration, his dimples deepen as the wide grin spreads across his face. "Stop it. When you smile at me, there's no way I can resist those dimples."

"You are so beautiful, Bridgette. I think I fell in love with you the first day I saw you at Celestial Manor."

"Yeah, I thought you were the most gorgeous man I had ever laid eyes on."

He states in a matter of fact tone, "I want to make us permanent."

"Permanent? We are permanent."

"No. I mean I want you to marry me," he says with a bit of nervousness in his voice. "I know lying in bed isn't the most romantic place to ask this question, but I'm asking anyway."

She sits up. "Asking me at all is romantic to me. I love you, Jason. With you being a part of my life these past months, I can't see my life without you anymore. Being with you is all I see when I see my future. I want you to move in with me when I move in to the house."

He searches her face questioning what those words mean. "Are you saying you won't marry me? You only want to live with me?"

"No. I'm not being clear. Yes. I will marry you Jason, but I want to be married at Celestial Manor before we open. That's months away. I'm moving in to the house next weekend. I want you to move in with me when I move in. I can't wait months to be with you."

He is so glad for those words, "Sure, that's a plan I can get on board with. We can have our wedding there before the grand opening."

She kisses him deeply. If Celeste's happiness depends on their love, then they will unite Edward and Celeste very soon.

Pulling her face away from kissing him, he says, "I love you Bridgette, with all of my heart."

"I love you, too, Jason. I think you are my destiny. The fact that everything has fallen into place for us, beginning with you looking like Edward to me looking like Celeste, it's already written for us. I heard a quote once that I always think about when I look into your eyes. It says the best kiss is the one that has been exchanged a thousand times between the eyes before it reaches the lips. Your eyes pulled me into your soul before you ever said a word. You had me at hello."

Jason's heart explodes. "Bridgette, my definition of perfect is you. Yes, you had me at hello, too. I saw you and I thought you were the most beautiful woman I had ever laid eyes on. With you, I couldn't get my heart to stop talking to my brain. I knew I had only just met you, but I was in love like a teenager. The statement of when you are really in love, you will know it, is true. I was in love long before you were with me."

"Jason, I was trying to play it safe, but every time I look into those blue eyes of yours, I throw caution to the wind. You have been, since I met you, my safe place."

Their lips meet in a long lingering kiss that seals their fate. Both relish in their love for each other. He moves over her kissing her passionately. As their desire sours, for the first time, they are truly making love, for both have now sealed it.

They are harmoniously indulging in ecstasy of a different kind. She relates her feelings to those she knew Edward and Celeste shared. She embraces him not only with her arms, but with her swollen heart. As she comes with an explosion, she hears him say, "You are my destiny."

CHAPTER 23

THEN COMES MARRIAGE

The next few weeks are busy for Bridgette and Jason. The house is complete, allowing Bridgette to move in the last weekend in August. She hires a moving company for the labor, choosing to pack her things on her own. She is so well prepared that the actual move is over within two hours. She spends the next week unpacking, and shopping for things she needs for the house. Her new furniture was delivered the same afternoon that she moved in. She's excited that everything is falling into place. The house is wonderful.

Jason follows her move with his. He gives her the week to get settled, then moves his things in on the next Saturday. He, too, is well prepared, so the move is quick and efficient. He doesn't bring a lot of his furniture, because it doesn't match the décor of the house. He takes a room on the second floor to make as his private man cave, and another for his office.

The following Friday night, Bridgette's father and Jason's parents are invited to dinner. The evening is pleasant, so they sit outside on the terrace. The sunset cascades over the mountains with an orange and yellow glow. The peaceful atmosphere gives Bridgette pause as she thanks her lucky stars to have such a wonderful life. She loves Jason's parents. His parents seem to like her as well. She can tell he is close to his family. His father, Jason, and her father are off in the corner laughing and shooting the breeze. His mother sits beside Bridgette on a chaise next to her. She looks at Bridgette, "You make my son very happy."

Somewhat surprised at the comment, she replies to his mother, "He has made me very happy as well."

His mother says, "I've never seen him so at peace. He used to be all about his business with no personal life to mention. Now, we can't get him to talk about anything else but you."

Bridgette watches Jason and smiles taking in his mother's praise. Looking at his mother, Bridgette says, "It was so crazy how we found each other. If it weren't for Celestial Manor, we would have never met. That's why it means so much to me. I credit this place for leading me to my future."

Jason's mother looks at the Manor in clear view of where they sit. "It is a beautiful place. Its regal stature will most definitely bring in great business for you. Have you begun advertising yet? It will be ready in a few weeks, right?"

"Yes, but Jason and I want to get married there first."

His mother is pleased. "I knew he had asked you, but hadn't heard of any definite dates."

"We are planning to wed in three weeks."

Excited, Jason's mother says, "I couldn't be happier for you two."

"Mrs. Cranston. I love your son very much. I want you to know I will spend the rest of my life trying to make him happy."

"Bridgette, call me Beth. She continues, Jason was not eager to settle down. When he was younger, girls would call the house all the time for him. The girls were calling his brother as well. His brother jumped in, but Jason wasn't the least bit interested. He just wasn't ready until you came along. He was all business. His brother and sister found love and family, but I was beginning to worry about Jason. He was doing the playboy thing a little too much for my taste. There were never attachments in his life. I want him to settle down and be happy. I can rest now that he has found you. All of my children are creating their own families, and that makes me happy."

Bridgette laughs. "Sorry to laugh, but you sound like a playbook from my father's expectations for me. He'd always ask when I was going to find someone and settle down. I kept telling him when I finished law school, so I guess I didn't lie after all."

His mother eagerly tells her, "Let me know if you need any help with the wedding plans."

Bridgette looks surprised, "Okay. I'm letting you know now. I do need your help if you are really offering."

His mother gets very excited. "Jason's brother and sister didn't involve me at all in their wedding plans. I would be very happy to assist."

They set up a day during the week to go try on wedding dresses and order the cake. Even though it will be an elegant wedding, she doesn't want to make it too large. His mother reminds her of the business they are in. She is willing to bet the guest list may get pretty large. Her father being a doctor, and Jason and his father in the same business will add guests quickly. Bridgette acknowledges that it's a possibility, but sticks by her desire to keep it small.

On Monday morning, Bridgette is set to do a final run through on Celestial Manor with the contractors. Since she has been closely involved all along, she expects no issues. Walking into the entryway, she is dazzled with the result. They do a run-through of everything. She sees nothing that she opposes for signing off. She takes the pen and signs each document. After the crew leaves, Jason and Bridgette walk through again. It is bittersweet since she has gotten used to being here every day involved in the remodeling.

Jason says his good-byes and heads off to work. Bridgette stays to begin the planning for setting up each location. Furniture and paintings are due to arrive tomorrow. She has scheduled almost everything for the same day. She hopes she hasn't made a mistake doing that. It could get overwhelming.

She walks into Celeste's room. She has kept this room as the Penthouse suite. She has styled it in the same design as it was in 1912. The furniture had arrived on Friday for this room, so it was the first to be completed. Based on the pictures she had of the room, she ordered the exact style of furniture with the same engraved design on the posts and bureau. It is so beautiful with its matching bedding and curtains. The lighting in the room is perfect. She sighs with pleasure at the picturesque scene.

"It is beautiful, isn't it?"

Startled, she turns quickly to see Celeste. "Do you like it Celeste?"

Celeste reviews the room and with a sweet sigh, says "Yes."

"I'm so glad you like it. I tried to get it to look exactly like you had it."

"You did a wonderful job."

Bridgette asks, "How are you, Celeste?"

"Bridgette, it is time to help me find Edward. Can you do that?"

"Celeste, you said that if love is here, you thought Edward would return to you. Jason loves me. We are together now."

"Then why is there no Edward?"

Feeling she has no answer, she doesn't try to make one up. "I don't know Celeste. I have never dealt with death and how it works. Why are you stuck here, but Edward is not?"

Celeste cries, "I could have left. The light came, but I didn't see Edward."

"Do you ever see the light now? Can you call on it to come back?"

Celeste's face saddens. "It does not hear me anymore. I think Jason may be Edward, so he cannot come back to me."

Unwilling to accept that, Bridgette says, "I don't believe that, Celeste. I think if Jason were Edward, Edward would never allow me to marry him. He would be here for you."

Looking at Bridgette, she nods in agreement. "How do we know?"

"I don't know, Celeste. I need to do some research on life after death. What happens to a soul when it goes to the light? I have been hoping that Edward will show while Jason and I are getting married. It will bring love back in these hallowed halls."

"I hope so, Bridgette. My sadness grows deeper each passing day." A tear flows down Celeste's face. First one tear, then another one, she cannot hold them back anymore. She falls on to the bed and sobs.

Bridgette is heart-broken. She goes to her wanting to wrap her arms around her. "How can I help you Celeste? What can I do?"

"I just want to be with Edward." As Celeste completes those words, she disappears.

Bridgette leaves Celestial Manor down-hearted. She has no idea how to help her. Why doesn't Edward love her enough to come? Can't he see her pain?

Bridgette leaves to run errands, just missing Jason. He came back to give her the floor plans, contracts, and licenses they had signed to begin the new business. When he doesn't see Bridgette, he decides to search in Celeste's room before leaving.

When he walks in, he sees Celeste sitting in the chair in front of the window.

Celeste turns to see Jason. When she spots him, she doesn't perceive him as Jason, she sees Edward. "Edward, my love, you are here."

He is confused at first. He has communicated with her over and over. Why doesn't she know he is not Edward? Not wishing to upset her he concedes, "It's okay, Celeste. Everything is okay."

"Edward, what has taken you so long to return to me? I have waited so long for you."

She is very excited. As she gets closer to him, Jason becomes disoriented. He tries to mumble something, but can't get it out. He feels faint. Blackness envelopes him as he falls to the floor.

Bridgette arrives home at six. Jason is usually there by five, so it surprises her that he is not at home. She dials his number, but it goes to voicemail. She decides to shower before dinner.

By eight o'clock, Bridgette gets concerned. She has been calling him for the last hour. Her gut tells her something is wrong. She walks out on the front porch thinking she will see him coming down the drive. It was then that she sees his Mercedes in front of Celestial Manor. She runs to his car but doesn't see him. She repeatedly calls his name when she enters. She runs upstairs and sees a light coming from Celeste's room. She walks in to see Jason lying on the floor. She runs to him.

Celeste says, "Leave him alone. I am trying to show him that he is Edward."

Bridgette almost in tears now yells back at Celeste, "No, he is not Edward! Celeste, I am begging you, please don't hurt Jason."

Celeste demands, "He is not Jason. He is Edward. I would never hurt Edward."

Celeste looks torn between her great, great grand-daughter, and the man on the floor. "Bridgette, I would never hurt him. I love him."

Bridgette begins yelling at Jason to wake up. She pats him on the face to stir him. Slowly, he begins to arouse as Celeste lets go.

Disoriented, Jason moans, "Bridgette, what's going on?" Trying to sit up, his head begins to spin.

Bridgette pushes Jason up and fumes at Celeste. "I am taking him home. I trusted you Celeste." She helps Jason to his feet and gets him to the elevator. As the door closes Celeste stands in front of it crying.

Bridgette gets Jason in his car and drives him to the house. She helps him inside. He falls on to the couch unable to support his own weight. "Are you alright Jason?"

"Yes, I'm fine. Bridgette, Celeste was trying to show me that I'm Edward. They loved each other so much. It was as if I was Edward. I felt his love for her. It was just as powerful as our love."

Bridgette doesn't know how to respond to this. "So, you don't think she was trying to hurt you?"

"No, not at all, she was trying to see if I was, in fact, Edward. I think she knows now that I'm not."

She kisses and hugs him. "Jason, this has scared me. I don't know if I can run a business out of a place that is haunted. She may show herself to others in the future. If we can't bring Edward back, she is stuck."

Jason looks at her and concedes this may be the truth. "I feel so sorry for her, Bridgette. I feel like I love her."

Confused, she says, "What?"

"I am perplexed right now, but I was Edward just now. I knew his love for her. I recognized it."

"Jason, I did too, but it was through the eyes of Celeste. Don't confuse the two."

Jason sits up now feeling better. "Bridgette, there is something here. We need to help her. I don't know how, but we have to."

Bridgette leans back on the couch feeling frustrated and lost. "We have tried, Jason. What do we need to do to help her cross over?"

"I have no idea, but it's time we found out."

The next few weeks in between wedding arrangements, they agree to go see a spiritual advisor. A spiritual advisor and a priest should know how to free Celeste. They agree it will happen after the wedding.

CHAPTER 24

WEDDING SURPRISE

The next few weeks are full of plans and activities in and out of Celestial Manor. Getting set up for the wedding has consumed Bridgette's time. The morning of the wedding, Bridgette meets with the wedding planner one last time. The caterers, florist, and the wedding cake arrive as scheduled. Bridgette goes off with her bridesmaids and family to dress for her special day. As she puts on her wedding dress, she is overwhelmed with emotion.

Choosing the dress is always supposed to be difficult for the bride, but Bridgette saw the dress the minute she walked into the bridal shop. Hanging on a mannequin, she saw the drape and fit was exactly what she wanted. The dress, with its lace neck and arms and satin bodice billowing into a full train, is exquisite. It's the visual fantasy she had always dreamed of for her perfect wedding. Trying on no other, she selects and pays for the gown within an hour of arrival. Jason's mother is astonished at her decisiveness. Providing delivery directions, they leave the shop relieved that the biggest task she needs to do is now complete.

Examining herself in the mirror, she is glowing. The wow's and ah's being delivered from her bridesmaids help to assure her that the dress selection was a decision well made. The calm she has about marrying Jason confirms her decision to take this wonderful man as her husband.

He spends the last night at his place. He has rented his house out, with tenants moving in next month. The furniture is still there, so he is able to stay the night with no problem. His belongings are already moved to Bridgette's. He just needs to pack an overnight bag. He'd had his best man (his father), and friends over last night for a manly celebration while Bridgette's friends surprise her with a bridal shower. With such short notice for their friends, everything has been kept small and intimate.

As time ticks away, their vows loom near. The groomsmen pat Jason on the back and tell him they will see him at the hanging. Jason laughs. With much anticipation, his nerves are slightly edgy. His dad sees the anxiety, "Are you okay, Jason?"

"Sure, dad."

"You are looking pale and a little stressed. Are you having second thoughts?"

"No, of course not, dad, she is the woman of my dreams."

His father replies, "Jason, your face is white as a sheet. Are you sure you're okay?"

"Yeah, dad, can you give me a minute alone? I'll be down in a minute."

After his father leaves, he turns to Celeste. "Celeste, what are you doing here now?"

Celeste is looking at him with sadness. "Edward, why can't you come to me?"

Jason is rattled now, realizing her state of panic. "I am not Edward, Celeste."

Celeste refuses to hear his words. "I know you are Edward. Edward would not leave me alone like this. That is why you have come to me." She speaks not to Jason, but into him as if she is speaking to Edward. "Edward, it is time to come to me now. I cannot go on." She begins to cry. She rushes to Jason. As she comes forward, he feels faint and falls to the floor. Celeste kneels to him, and speaks to Edward. "Edward, I cannot let you marry another woman. You are mine, forever."

Jason lays there in a cloud of uncertainty. He wants to get up, but finds he can't move. He hears Celeste in the distance, but can't make out her words. The more he panics, the weaker he gets. He sees another blurred image, but can't make it out.

Everyone is now in position for the wedding to begin downstairs. Bridgette is just leaving her room to position herself behind the doors that lead to the ballroom where the ceremony is to take place. Guests have all been seated by the groomsmen. Standing in front near the pastor, the groomsmen are surprised that Jason hasn't come down yet. His father, who is his best man, gets concerned. Remembering Jason's condition when he left, it was not a good sign that had not come down. Excusing himself, he goes through the doors that lead to the back entryway for upstairs. When he arrives, he sees Jason on the floor. He runs to him and tries to rouse him. Jason is unresponsive. Forgetting about the bride in the hall, he runs down stairs in a panic and yells, "Get a doctor."

Bridgette, who had been calm up to this point, asks, "What's wrong?"

"It's Jason. He's passed out."

Bridgette yells for someone to go get her father, leaving her bridal party to go upstairs. She heads straight to Celeste's room. Entering, she sees that Celeste is hovering over Jason. "What did you do to Jason, Celeste?"

Celeste stands glaring at her. "It is not Jason. It's Edward. Can't you see it, Bridgette? You cannot marry him. He is mine."

Bridgette tries to run to Jason, but is blocked by Celeste. "Let me help him, Celeste. He will not be good to you if he dies." Trying to scare Celeste, she tells her, "He will be just like Edward. He will leave you if you take him this way."

Celeste sees Jason lying on the floor. "Please forgive me Bridgette. I cannot let go of him."

Bridgette pleads with her to let go.

Everyone in the room is staring at Bridgette like she is crazy until they see the ghostly image of Celeste suspended over Jason. The fright in their faces is evident for all to see. Jason's father enters the room with Bridgette's father. When her father sees the situation, he is horrified. Jason had casually mentioned a ghost in these hallowed halls, but he never thought it to be true. Moving to Bridgette, Jason's father says, "What the hell is going on here?"

Bridgette turns to see the horror of Jason's fathers face. "Just give me a minute. I think I can get to her." Her father steps forward and it gives her an idea. She turns back to Celeste, "Celeste, my father is here to look after Edward. Will you let him help Edward?" Her father stares at Bridgette in disbelief.

Celeste who is scared now says, "I want to, but I can't let you near him. You will take him away from me."

Bridgette moves slowly closer. "No, I will not take him Celeste. Please, just let the doctor see to him. If you love him, you will not want to hurt him."

Celeste says, "I do love him. I have always loved him."

"Then let the doctor look after him. Okay?"

Celeste moves slightly to the side of Jason. Dr. Chandler runs over putting his finger on Jason's wrist to find his pulse, he announces, "His pulse is shallow."

Bridgette begins to beg Celeste. "Please Celeste, don't hurt Edward. I know you love him, and would never intentionally hurt him, so please don't do it now. If you don't let go of him soon, he will die."

Celeste begins crying. "I don't want Edward to die again, but I can't be with him until he does. He will want you."

Bridgette knows this is the pivotal moment when her words could save Jason's life. "I will call off the wedding if you want. I will leave and let you have him forever."

Through tears, Celeste asks, "You will leave?"

Bridgette choking back the tears herself, says, "If saving him will make you let go, I will." Bridgette knows that although she is saying these words to pacify Celeste, she knows Celeste will not let go of Jason. She believes he is Edward. Bridgette fears Jason's life will be committed to a ghost, because she will never allow anyone near Jason.

Celeste backs away from Jason. "Okay, I will release him." As she backs away, Jason begins to groggily wake up.

Relieved, Bridgette stays where she is. She doesn't want to panic Celeste. Jason's father and Dr. Chandler help Jason stand up. To everyone's surprise, Jason speaks sweetly to her. "Celeste, I'm here for you. I have spoken to Edward. He waits for you."

Celeste places both hands over her mouth in disbelief. "You did? What did he say?"

"He will speak to you now." He begins searching the room, "Edward, please show yourself." He explains to the group, while I was in the suspended state, I could see around the room. Edward was there. It was a pale shadow of him, but he was there. Edward looks so distraught seeing Celeste's state.

Edward does not appear. Jason in panicked voice says, "Edward, you are here. I saw you. Please come forward and show yourself."

Edward replies, "I have never been able to show myself. I don't know why, but I can't. I have been here all along, but I could not tell Celeste I was here. She could not see me."

Jason explains, "Edward, use all of your strength and the memory of your life with Celeste. Use those memories to bring yourself into view. You can do it, Edward. I know you can. I just saw you myself."

Edward looks at Celeste. Before his eyes, she is the beautiful woman he married the day of their wedding. He remembers their first night together and the love they shared as husband and wife. As he does so, he slowly becomes visible to those in the room. He is captured by Celeste's beauty. He willed himself back to the day they married.

Celeste is shocked to see him. She runs to him and cries in his arms. He holds her tightly. He pulls her back, kissing her face and her sweet lips. Words of love are spilling everywhere. The glow of their love is palpable between them.

Jason moves to Bridgette who is now crying. She embraces Jason and thanks him for helping the two come together. "Bridgette, I didn't do it. Edward did. He has been here all along trying to reach her. When I was in my suspended state, he spoke to me and asked me to help him get to her. Their love along with ours gave him the strength."

Edward and Celeste are facing Bridgette and Jason. Edward says, "Jason, I have watched you and Bridgette. Your love for one another is as deep as mine and Celeste's love." He looks at Bridgette and stares. "You look so much like Celeste. You are my great, great grand-daughter. You are beautiful." Glancing toward Celeste, then back to Bridgette he says, "You took after the better side of our family." He bends down kissing Celeste on the forehead and says, "Thank you for taking such good care of Celeste since your arrival here. When you came to Celestial Manor, it made me very happy. It gave me hope again. I was always present when you were with her. It gave me some peace to know she had found you. I was happy to see you, but also pleased that Celeste had someone and was no longer alone. It hurt me that she was in so much pain. I know now my error. I was so focused on our pain. I didn't focus on our love. That's why I couldn't show myself. The answer was love. The love Jason showed me just now."

Jason responds, "I'm so glad I could see you Edward. Celeste, you did the right thing by taking me. We would never have found Edward if you hadn't. Your desire for him made you go to any lengths to get back to him." He turns to Bridgette, "If Bridgette and I can love half as much as you and Edward, we will have a happily ever after."

Celeste looks at Bridgette, "I love you my dear, more than you will know. The day you came into my home is the day I found love again. You lessened my pain. I have focused on my pain from losing Edward for so long. When you came, and I took you back to my life, I began remembering our love again. I was not so focused on the hurt that has kept me from moving on."

The room begins to light up. In the corner of the room, a blinding light spills from the ceiling. It moves in the direction of Edward and Celeste. They stare toward the light, then at each other. Edward says, "It is time to go Celeste. Take my hand, and we will go to the light together." They move closer to the light, but Celeste pulls Edward's arm to stop. Celeste looks at Jason and says, "Love her Jason, just as Edward and I love each other. I am sorry if I hurt either of you." She looks up at Edward, and he nods his head yes. It's as if he can read her mind. With Edward's acknowledgement, Celeste says, "The two of you have our blessing." She turns to Bridgette. "You are a stunning bride."

Bridgette feels the tears falling down her face. Forgetting she has her wedding gown on, she smiles. "Thank you, Celeste. I love you both."

As the light envelops Edward and Celeste, Celeste turns to Bridgette and almost cries, "I will tell your mother how very much you love her." When the light retreats, they are gone.

CHAPTER 25

BRIDGING TIME

Bridgette turns to Jason, "Are you alright?"

"Yes, I felt very strange before, but I feel okay now."

She turns to her father, "Dad, can you go down and tell everyone the wedding is postponed?"

Her father nods his head and turns to leave, but Jason interrupts. "Bridgette, why do you want to postpone it? I feel fine, are you having second thoughts?"

"No, of course not, but I feel like I need to give you time to think about all of this. My great, great grandmother just took possession of you. I would think you would be a little upset."

"Well, sure. It's not every day that I am possessed by a ghost, but that has nothing to do with the fact that I can't wait to be your husband."

Bridgette walks to him and puts her arms around his neck. She kisses him softly. Looking down at her gown she says, "Its bad luck to see the bride before the wedding."

Jason smiles, "I am not worried about luck. Fate is on our side."

Dr. Chandler takes Bridgette's hand, "Come on you two, let's get this wedding started."

After a few announcements to the wedding guests they apologize for the delay. The wedding begins.

Jason stands with his groomsmen at the front of the room. As Bridgette enters the aisle, he sees the most gorgeous woman he has ever met. Her hair is full of curls draped in layers. His mind goes to the fact that the hairstyle makes her look exactly like Celeste. The dress with its white billows of material cascading into a full train is spectacular. It lends support of an earlier time when women dressed with elegant long dresses. He smiles at her as her eyes meet his. Warmth and love swell his heart.

Bridgette can see the love in his eyes. She smiles at him. She too thinks about Celeste. It is understandable that Celeste thought he was Edward. His handsome dark features and sky blue eyes give credence to her confusion. Bridgette has never seen a man that makes her heart skip like this man does.

Taking her hand from her father, Jason promises her father that he will take good care of her. Dr. Chandler says, "Jason, I know you will."

They face the minister. While exchanging their vows, the lights flicker for a moment. Jason starts laughing, "She's at it again."

Bridgette laughs. She says, "I hope they are both witnessing our love."

He smiles, "I do too."

After the ceremony, they party with their high spirited guests. It is wonderful to see Victor. He loves the changes that have been made with the place. Since the death of Mr. Barkley, Bridgette and Victor have kept in touch and become close. He is so happy to see this joyous union. His best wishes are heartfelt and supportive.

She finds herself walking through the halls of Celestial Manor in pride. She goes to Celeste's room. Standing in silence, she waits for Celeste to appear, but she doesn't. Jason stands in the doorway watching Bridgette walk the room. She sees him and begins to cry.

"Honey, what's wrong?"

"I can tell she's gone. I'm going to miss her."

"It's okay to miss her. She's family."

Bridgette looks into his eyes and grins, "You are my family now."

"Yes I am, now and forever. Hey, not to cut this love fest short, but we have a plane to catch."

She says, "You have been very private about the plans."

He says, "I told you, you get to make all the decisions on the wedding. I get the honeymoon."

She kisses his lips softly. "Where are you taking me, Jason?"

He takes her hand and pulls her out of the room into hers, "Get changed into the outfit on your bed."

She wraps her arms around his neck and starts kissing him deeply. He struggles not to dive into that kiss, and take her in the room right then and there to consummate their marriage. He pulls away, "See you downstairs."

When Bridgette finishes dressing in the white below the knee skirt and matching jacket, she starts down the wide staircase. Waiting on her at the bottom of the steps are all the guests. She instructs all the free ladies to move to the bottom of the steps. She turns holding onto the handrails of the steps and throws the corsage backward. The screams from the women makes her turn quickly to see who catches it. Her best friend Nicki catches it. She moves down the staircase and through the guests to the limo parked out front. Her father is waiting to open the car door for her. She hugs him with an exaggerated squeeze. "I love you, dad."

"Love you too, honey. Have a wonderful time on your honeymoon."

Jason pulls her hand to get into the car. She turns to wave goodbye to her guests.

They get to the airport where Jason has rented a private plane. "Where are we going Jason?"

After buckling up, he fills her in with the details. "We are going to New York."

"New York? What made you decide on New York?"

Jason smiles and takes her hands in his. "We are staying at The Plaza Hotel, the same hotel that Edward and Celeste stayed at on their wedding night. I have even booked the same room."

Bridgette's eyes fill with tears. "Jason, you are the most perfect man. How did I get so lucky to find you?"

"Fate," he says with matter of fact in his voice.

They arrive at the New York airport at 7:00 pm. A limo is waiting. They make great time with traffic and arrive at the hotel by eight.

Edward carries her over the threshold, kissing her all the way. She pushes the door open to a room full of flowers. When Jason sets her down, she stops dead still. The room is exactly as she remembers. Having seen all of this when Celeste took her back

175

while in the coma, she is awe struck at the similarities. How could it be the same after all this time? Jason must have gone to great lengths to make this happen. "How did you get this room to look so much like before?"

Jason explains, "I was up in the attic at Celestial Manor and found some old pictures. There were old post cards of the hotel and their room. It was in their wedding album. They must have saved it for a souvenir of their honeymoon."

"Unbelievable," she says taking in everything.

Jason walks up behind her. Pulling her hair up, he kisses her on the back of her neck. She turns in his arms, and places an intense kiss on his lips. Their lips meet again and again, parting only to return into a deeper kiss. He begins backing her to the bed. She pulls away saying, "Wait, I brought a seductive gown. I need to put it on."

Groaning, he reluctantly says okay.

She searches for her luggage and realizes no one brought them up. She turns in panic to Jason and says, "Where is our luggage?"

"My things are in that bureau, your things are in the dressing room over there." He points to the closed door that she remembers from Celeste's wedding night.

She walks to the door. She opens it and sees all of her clothes hanging on a long bar inside an open door wardrobe closet. She turns to smile back at Jason. "You thought of everything."

He is slow to answer, but finally replies, "I try."

She enters the dressing room and closes the door. Taking off her suit, she grabs her seductive lingerie, and puts it on. The spaghetti straps hold the white low cut bra gown in place. She pulls the see through white robe over it. Removing the clips, she bends her head over, fluffing her hair. Looking in the mirror, she takes a deep breath as she sees her image is similar to Celeste. She sighs then, turns to open the door.

Jason has changed into a robe and pajama bottoms. He studies her when she enters the room. "My God you are beautiful!"

She gushes with excitement. Walking toward him she crooks her finger to motion him to come to her.

He beams a bad boy smile and walks toward her. He pulls her close, kissing her slowly searching her lips with his. Her arm goes up around his neck and pulls him in close. The heat between them intensifies. He removes her robe. Kissing her shoulders, then the nape of her neck, he pulls the spaghetti strap off her shoulder. Not wishing to stop there, he backs her away from him pulling his robe off discarding it. They fall onto the bed devouring each other with hot kisses and exploring touches.

Bridgette is burning with desire. She moans to him, "I want you." Her hands roam his body until she reaches his hardness.

He feels her hand and the heat of their bodies explode. It drives him over the edge. They consummate their marriage with frantic, enthusiastic love making. They are consumed with delirious passion. Each touch, each move, takes them to levels of ecstasy that wipes out the world around them. They are suspended in a fevered bliss that engulfs them beyond pleasure. They meet in an explosion of ecstasy, fulfillment and decadence. Afterward, both fall spent and satisfied.

He gazes at this woman who is now his wife. He is filled with so much love. He says, "I love you. I love you more this moment than I have ever loved you."

Her heart explodes. "I love you too, Jason."

"Jason, I have never been so happy. Tonight, I knew Edward's and Celeste's love." Looking up into his face she says, "I was brought to this earth to love you. I desire everything about you." She places her hand on his cheek. "I yearn for you. Not just to make love, but I love all of you. I see your handsome face and my heart skips a beat. I touch your hard body and I lose all sanity. I taste your kisses and I want more of you. I can't get enough. Each time we make love, I can't wait until the next time to do it again. I will always love you. I hope life supports our love and we don't have to lose each other like Celeste and Edward did. I'm sorry I keep bringing them up, but I know their love Jason. It was pure and committed. I want that same love for us."

"Bridgette, my love for you is just like Edward's is for Celeste. I say *is*, instead of was, because their love exists even today. Hell, we just saw them today. I watched Edward's pain as he tried to be seen. He suffered as long as she did. Celeste just didn't know it. Because of their tragedy, a bridge over time brought us together. Our love cements their gift of bringing us together. I am glad I look so much like Edward because without that, I would never have met you. That would have been another tragedy."

Two hearts were sealed the night of Bridgette and Jason's wedding. A gift was produced from a tragedy of love lost. Time however, didn't diminish the love that Edward and Celeste felt for one another. It cultivated a new love. As they close their eyes tonight, they know a love lost was found, and a love found will never be lost.

THE END

About The Author

Linda Mayo

Surprising to me is that I have completed a second novel. Taking a novel writing class was the beginning of an adventure of creativity, and the dream of laying words to paper. Driven by my own desire to design stories of everlasting love, my characters are visions of hope and happiness.

81494905R00099

Made in the USA
Lexington, KY
16 February 2018